DEDICATION

To my readers. Crafty. Crazy. Passionate.

This might be a good time to come clean. She'd let things go too far, and she was way, way out of her depth. "I'm sorry to tell you this, but Sampson hasn't been checking in."

"I figured as much."

Why didn't he seemed surprised? "Does this happen a lot?"

"No."

She stared up at his unshaved face, the shadows casting dramatic angles off the hard planes of his high cheekbones and masculine brow.

He added, "People disappear in our line of business. Hazard of the trade."

"You think he's dead?"

He shrugged, like it didn't matter one way or another.

"But doesn't that make things kind of *over?*" she asked.

"Over?" He chuckled bitterly.

"Sorry. But I'm new to the, uh, pest-control world. If the boss is gone, how doesn't that put a wrench in things?"

"I never said it didn't, but this work never ends."

She sensed a deeper meaning there; however, none of this was her problem. "Whatever. Fine. It's over for me," she said. "I quit."

"Jane, maybe Sampson left that part of the job description out, but you've been misinformed about your options. There is no *out*. There is no *quitting*."

"Sorry?"

"You know too much, and once you're in, you're in."

SHE'S GOT THE GUNS

A suite #45 novel.

M.O.

MACK

SHE'S
GOT THE
GUNS

CHAPTER ONE

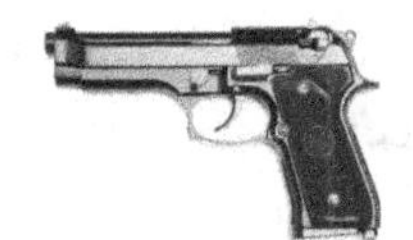

Emily Rockford sat anxiously behind the beat-up reception desk, with nothing to keep her company aside from the faded yellow wallpaper and the monotonous grinding sound of the AC unit. A unit that was crammed into a partially boarded-up window, had no off switch, and dribbled rust-brown sludge down the wall. She was pretty sure the grungy brown carpet underneath it was rotten, but what did that matter?

This office is a shithole, she thought. *And why would anyone hardwire the AC to run nonstop?* Granted, they were in Texas and, like today, the weather could get unbearably hot. But no off switch? No way to unplug it?

Very strange, she thought.

Then again, nothing about this situation felt right. Not the terms of her employment, not this abandoned, run-down strip mall, and certainly not the fact there was no business name posted anywhere. The only thing identifying this office was the "Suite #45" painted outside in chunky black letters above the frosted-glass door.

What the hell were they *really* selling here? Mr. Sampson, the man who'd hired her, said they performed "discreet pest control" for the sort of people who didn't want their neighbors knowing they had roach issues. "It's a status thing," he'd said.

But this was El Paso, Texas, not Beverly Hills. People were more caught up with everyday life than what their neighbors thought. It was why she'd moved here. Lack of *noseys*.

Emily hugged her pilling white cardigan to her shivering body. Any second now, she would have to bust open the AC's front panel and shut off that icebox. The only reason she hadn't yet was out of respect for Mr. Sampson, who didn't vibe as friendly. At least not over the phone. She hadn't actually met the guy, despite three days passing since she'd started work. "Work" being a term she used loosely here. All she did was sit and wait for the phone to ring.

It never did.

Then, at the end of each shift, she found one hundred dollars deposited into her Zelle account, just as they'd agreed over the phone.

Well, the man did say he might be late coming in to train me. Only, she'd thought he meant hours, not days.

Emily got up from her creaky chair, one of those antique oak things with metal wheels and ass-shaped grooves carved into the seat. With body heat on her mind, she started walking circles around the small, nearly empty office that contained three beige filing cabinets against the back wall, her prison-gray desk made of sheet metal (nothing in the drawers), and a grimy Mr. Coffee. The thing had at least an inch of scale caked inside the carafe. *Nasty.*

She glanced at the machine, noting a giant cockroach skittering across the yellow Formica counter off to the side of the room. It stopped, turned in her direction as if warning her off, and then disappeared down the rust-stained sink at the end.

She lifted a brow. *Pest control, huh?* Well, if that was really Mr. Sampson's business, he sucked at it. The lack of customers was a huge hint, too.

With the blood now flowing again, Emily walked back to the desk and checked her cell for the fiftieth time. Still no new emails from Sampson.

This is insane. Where was he? Why hire her to just sit around and do nothing? She replayed their one and only phone conversation in her mind: "The key to the front door will be taped under the doormat. Keep it safe with you at all times. You are to answer the phone and take messages. No questions. Ever. No conversations. Ever. Just take the message, hang up. If I'm not in the office, place the message in the top drawer of the desk. That's it."

"I think I can handle that," she'd said, knowing full well the entire situation was shady as fuck. But she had to pay rent. She had to eat. The challenge was, employment options were limited for people like her—no real skills, no references, no college education. Ed had never allowed her to work or take classes. Moving to El Paso was supposed to be the first step to a fresh start. Unfortunately, after two weeks she'd already burned through the small amount of cash she'd managed to scrape together before running.

New identities cost a lot.

The red push-button phone on her desk began blaring with a high-pitched ring, making her jump in her black flats.

"Sonofa…" She pressed her palm over her heart. She'd never actually heard the damned thing make a noise until now. Not a soul had passed through the door either.

She reached for the handpiece, not knowing what to expect. "He-hello?"

"Tell Sampson," said a cold, gravelly voice, "customer ninety-two's rat has been taken care of."

His voice sent a chill down her spine. *I bet he killed the poor critter just by talking to it.* She grabbed the pad of legal paper on her desk and wrote down the message. Should she tell the caller that Mr. Sampson was MIA?

No. She shouldn't get involved. She was there to take messages from ten a.m. to four p.m. Monday through Friday. That was it. The less she knew about whatever this place really was, the better.

"Got it," she said, "and may I say who's calling?"

There was a long, static-filled pause. "Who the fuck is this?"

Shit. She wasn't supposed to ask questions. "My name is…*Jane.* I just started working here." She wasn't about to give him her name, even if Emily Rockford was an alias. She didn't have another two grand to buy another identity that came with a social security card and an Illinois driver's license of a twenty-six-year-old woman who vaguely resembled her: five-five height, Caucasian, green eyes, brown hair, and one hundred and thirty pounds.

"Well, *Jane,*" the man said in a bone-chilling voice, "I suggest you shut your fucking mouth and pass along the message." The line went dead.

Emily hung up and released a slow breath. She had a very bad feeling about this job. Very bad. But until she found something else, this was better than sleeping in the gutter. Or worse, next to Ed.

CHAPTER TWO

Wearing her only set of PJs—a lame yellow duckie T-shirt combo with matching shorts that she'd found in the 99-cent bin at Goodwill—Emily spent the long muggy night tossing and turning with wave after wave of internal debate.

That voice in her sour stomach screamed not to go back to that office in the morning. Unfortunately, her stomach kept being overruled by necessity, including the need to find a less dumpy apartment. It was bad enough that used needles littered the walkway just outside her door each morning, but she couldn't even get a decent night's sleep. The couple next door spent most nights drinking and fighting. Their cruel words—*"You're nothing. You're a stupid whore. I should kill you!"*—reminded her of the existence she'd left behind. Except, in the here and now, the yelling made her anxious. Back home, the yelling had given her a sick kind of relief.

Emily rolled to her side. It was painful to look back and know it had taken almost three years to grow a pair and leave Ed, but there hadn't been a day when she didn't think about running. Some days were better than others, like the days when Ed came home from work and spewed the most vile, hateful things. Those were the good days. Yelling didn't leave bruises. It was when Ed turned silent that she had to worry. Those were the bad days.

Never again. She rolled to her other side, the phantom ache of a once cracked rib throbbing against the mattress. *Put it out of your mind. You're free now.* She stared at the orange-and-black striped pattern on her window, a product of blinds that didn't close properly and the street-lamps just outside.

I really have to find a better place. But that wasn't a priority. She needed to save every dime she could. It was June, and the fall semester at the junior college would be starting in September. She planned to get her certificate in one impossible backbreaking semester and then get a job as a bookkeeper. A safe home with respectable employment was all she needed.

Patience and hard work. I can get there. Besides, no turning back now. Ed would kill her if he tracked her down. This path, as difficult as it might be, was the only way.

By nine a.m. the next morning, she'd gone for a three-mile run, showered, and dressed in one of the three outfits she'd purchased from the thrift store. Solid-color blouses and black skirts. Modest, unnoticeable. She'd even dyed her red hair to a chestnut brown. Emily Rockford was someone you'd look at and not really see. Utterly forgettable.

The old, pathetic her had worn flowery dresses and strappy leather sandals. The old her was expected to look cute to please Ed, especially when his friends came over to play poker. *Total assholes.* They would wait until Ed was too drunk to notice anything but the cards in his hands, and corner her in the kitchen. They'd grab her ass and breasts. The one time she'd tried to tell Ed about how they treated her, she got blamed and ended up with a black eye.

"Stop acting like a slut, and they'll stop treating you like one," he'd said.

Never again. Never again would she dress up if she didn't want to. Never again would she allow a person's hands on her like that.

Now wearing a navy blue blouse and a black skirt, with her unremarkable brown hair in a ponytail, Emily caught the bus for work and ended up arriving a few minutes early, so she ran across the street to the gas station. There was no bathroom in the office that she saw, and if there was one somewhere in the vacant strip mall, she doubted she'd want to use it.

She purchased a bottle of water and a small bag of pretzels, the cheapest things she could find, and hugged them to her chest as she jogged back, weaving through the logjam of cars stopped at the light.

Panting, she stepped up on the sidewalk and noticed a man—tall, lanky, dark hair—standing just outside the suite. He wore brown pants, a white shirt, and black dress shoes. *The outfit of a person who doesn't want to draw attention.* Just like her.

Could that be Mr. Sampson? But he looked too young, maybe thirtyish. Mr. Sampson had the gruff voice of a much older man.

Emily cautiously approached, noting the guy's sweaty face and shifty dark eyes. "Hi. Are you waiting for..." *No questions. No questions.* "I'm Jane, the receptionist." She held out her free hand.

He nodded but didn't take it. "I was told to come here and leave my message." He gave her his back, waiting for her to unlock the door.

Okay... Who showed up at an office to "leave a message"? Why not call? Why not text or email Mr. Sampson?

"Mind hurrying? I got things to do," the man urged.

Now it was her turn to have shifty eyes. Was anyone else around to hear her scream if this guy pulled something?

There wasn't.

All she had was the passing cars behind her, made up of people on their way south of the border to work at one of the factories, most of them distracted by their phones and traffic. Besides, who could hear anything over the constant roar of semis going north, carrying goods out of Mexico?

"One sec. Let me get the key." She slid her hand into her oversized black purse, making sure she'd brought her pepper spray. It was right where she wanted it, in that little pocket meant for her cell. "Here it is." She produced the key and opened the front door. The man followed her in.

"Why's it so cold?" he asked.

She headed straight to her desk, avoiding eye contact. Whoever this man was, whatever business he had with Mr. Sampson, it felt safer not to remember his face.

"Um, yeah. I think the AC's busted. Won't shut off." She set down her items from the gas station but kept her purse slung on her shoulder for easy reaching.

"Guess it's better than the alternative: no AC at all. Looks like it's going to be a scorcher today."

They were getting perilously close to having a conversation—against Mr. Sampson's rules.

She nodded and grabbed her pencil, making sure to put the desk between her and the man.

"Ready."

He slid an envelope from his back pocket and set it on the desk.

This was his message?

Now she *had* to look at him. He seemed to expect her to say or do something with it. But what? "Um. Thank you. I'll put this here." *I don't see you. I will not remember the scar on your upper lip or the color of your dark eyes.* She opened the top drawer and deposited the envelope. "I'll be sure your message is given to Mr. Sampson."

He narrowed his eyes. "That's it? I hand you fifty thousand to take care of my pest problem, and we're done?"

Fifty thousand? That was a lot of money just to kill a rat or take care of some roaches. Now she had zero doubt that Mr. Sampson *was* in the extermination business—the human kind.

Hell, maybe she'd known it the moment she walked in here, but before this, there was a plausible deniability angle. And she'd been hungry. After today, she couldn't look the other way, and she wasn't about to get caught up with someone even shadier than Ed. *I need to get the hell out of here.*

"I'm sorry. I'm just the receptionist. I take messages. Nothing more." Emily forced a polite smile to her lips, wanting the man to leave so she could quickly do the same.

"So when's Sampson coming, then?"

A very good question. "I just take messages," she repeated. *No conversations. No questions. Please go.*

"Fine. Tell him to call Rick ASAP." He pressed the tip of his index finger to the top of the desk. "And this job had better be done by Saturday like he promised."

It was Thursday. She had no clue if the job would get done or if she could deliver the message. Basically, she couldn't promise him anything.

Her stomach knotted into a nauseating lump. There was a part of her—a big, sick, damaged part—that didn't want to displease this guy. Ed had beaten the fear of men into her. It ran cold through her veins like a nightmare spiked with broken glass. It smelled of stale urine, from when she'd pissed herself after being tied up in a closet for two days.

She blinked up at Rick, willing the pleasant smile to stay put. "Of course. I'll give him the message."

Rick stared for a long moment, his right eye twitching, before he finally turned and left.

"Jesus." She tilted her head back toward the water-stained ceiling. Yesterday, this place felt like rock bottom, but little had she known there was a trapdoor beneath her feet, waiting to take her lower. It was time to go.

She eyed the drawer. *Fifty thousand. Fifty*

thousand dollars. If she worked five days a week for the next year, the most she could pull in was twenty-six thousand. She knew because she'd been obsessing over money. How much could she make? Was it enough to pay rent and tuition? Screw grocery shopping. She could go to the food bank or hit the dollar store once a day. A person could live off of peanut butter crackers, baked beans, Vienna sausages, ramen, and that fake orange drink crap with vitamin C. Sure, she'd die of a heart attack at forty years old, but forty was better than twenty-five—her current age.

"Forty." She chuckled bitterly and shoved her water and pretzels into her oversized purse. "At this rate, I'll be lucky to make it to thirty." Ed would never stop looking. He wouldn't rest until she was dismembered, the pieces placed in ten different suitcases and sprinkled across one hundred and thirty miles of New Jersey coastline. Add to that threat her uncanny ability to pick the most dangerous people to connect herself with and an early death was a sure thing.

She headed for the front door and was about to reach for the handle when the door jerked open. Startled, Emily gasped and looked up, locking eyes with the tall man blocking her path. He looked to be in his early thirties. He had tanned skin, unkempt black hair, and a sturdy build. His clothes—faded jeans, heavy military-style boots, and a black T-shirt that hugged his broad chest—said he was the type who *wanted* to be noticed, that he'd fuck you up if you messed with him. His soulless gray eyes said he wouldn't give a shit if you cried about it when he did.

"Where the hell is my money?" he said with a scratchy, deep voice.

It was him, the man who'd called yesterday and told her to shut the fuck up.

She didn't like being spoken to that way, but out of self-preservation, Emily pushed the anger down a deep dark hole inside her mind where she kept all the bad stuff. It was getting pretty crowded in there.

"I'm sorry. I'm just the receptionist. I answer the phone. I take messages. That's it," she said, praying that he too would just leave. There'd be no hope if he wanted to hurt her, which she assumed he would if he didn't get his way. She knew the type. *Dangerous.*

He narrowed those gray eyes. "Get Sampson on the phone."

"I'm sorry," she repeated, her voice as level as she could make it, "I just take messages."

"You're fucking telling me you can't call him?"

She shook her head no.

He stepped forward, forcing her back against the desk, the front door closing behind him. He leaned down so she had a clear view of the displeasure in his eyes. "He knows the rules. He knows the consequences. If I leave here without my money, I'll be forced to put a bullet in someone's head. And, just in case you're wondering, I only plan to stay for sixty seconds." He reached one arm behind him.

She guessed he had a gun back there. *Dangerous. Why did I have to be right about him?* Maybe it was one of the few perks of her past life—she could now spot an Ed from a mile away.

"I want. My fifty. Thousand," he added.

Fifty. Fifty. Her hands shaking, she slipped around to the other side of the desk and yanked open the drawer. "Here. Take it." She slid the envelope toward him.

He snagged it, looked inside, and offered a snarl. "Tell Sampson to call me. Next time I have to come looking for my money, I'll be going to his home, not his office."

She watched the man leave, noting the huge gun shoved in the waistband of his jeans at the small of his back.

I'm so done here. Whatever this place was, whatever services they provided, she was not having any of it.

She waited a minute, to ensure the guy was gone, and then walked outside, locked the door, and threw the key under the mat. Tomorrow she would start combing the job ads, but she was never coming back to this place.

CHAPTER THREE

Emily had no idea what would happen if she simply stopped showing up to suite forty-five. There had been no agreement with Mr. Sampson, verbal or otherwise, concerning the length of her employment. And, as far as he was concerned, she knew nothing about the real nature of his business. He would probably assume she'd shown up, saw the dump of an office, and decided it wasn't for her. If he did turn out to be upset over her departure, well, too bad. Luckily, he didn't know where she lived. All Sampson had was her name—the Emily Rockford one—and the email attached to her Zelle account. There was no way to track her down.

Why are you worried? she asked herself. The man had disappeared. Dead. Hiding. On the run. She didn't know which, but there was no reason to work herself up over quitting. She'd simply put a block on her Zelle account so that no more payments came through.

Done.

She spent Friday and most of the weekend filling out job applications anywhere that wouldn't be too nosy when it came to background checks—waitress at the hole-in-the-wall a few blocks down, cocktail server at the dive bar near the border crossing where the truckers liked to hang out, and car wash attendant.

There were plenty of jobs for those wanting to keep a low profile, but the problem with El Paso was its abundance of people just like her. Mexico was an arm's reach away, and while most people were simply passing through and heading north, some were as broke and desperate as she was. They couldn't afford to go anywhere else, so they kept their heads down, found whatever work they could, and then bought a ride out of town with one of the guys they called *pajaros*—birds to fly them away. In a car, of course. Airplanes required ID. Buses weren't a good option this close to the border. (Too frequently stopped by Border Patrol.)

All these little facts came from her meticulous internet research conducted during short stints to the public library near her old house in Jersey. Ten minutes here, five minutes there, while coming or going to the grocery store so as not to rouse Ed's suspicion. "Just checking out a book on gardening." Or, "Just returning my book on gardening," she'd say. It took over a year to examine prospective towns and plan her getaway, the biggest hurdle being that Ed kept a tight leash on money. She had gotten good at buying small things and returning them for cash. Socks, pens, conditioner that didn't work, a BBQ grilling set, wine that had gone "bad"—you name it, she figured out how to return it for cash.

As for her logic behind choosing El Paso when she might've fared better elsewhere, somewhere quiet and remote like a few towns she'd scouted in North Dakota, it was simple. Ed had connections. He knew how to find people.

At least in this country.

A place like El Paso gave her somewhere to run if it ever came to that. From Mexico, she could keep going south. She could disappear forever.

Of course, that wasn't her plan. She wasn't done with Ed just yet. A bad man like him had to pay for the things he'd done and still did.

Only a matter of time. Patience and planning.

Early Monday morning, after a good sleep that left her head clear but her ears itchy from using wadded-up toilet paper as earplugs, she put on her black shorts, a light gray tee, and tennis shoes to go for a quick run before the sun came all the way up. She grabbed her credit card and ID and slid them into her bra. She would stop by the drugstore on the way back and buy more brown hair dye. Red roots were not conducive to hiding one's identity. Looking average was the key—average height, common hair color, plain clothes. The only thing that stood out were her bright green eyes—her father's eyes.

She stepped outside onto the concrete walkway that edged a row of carports where tarry black pools dotted the empty spaces. She shoved her key into the deadbolt and—

"Hello, Jane," said an unhappy baritone voice.

Her heart jarred against her rib cage. For one split second, she thought it was Ed coming to collect on his dismemberment-suitcase promise, but the voice wasn't his. Neither was the tall, lanky body with the sweaty brow and scar on the upper lip.

Rick. "What are you doing here?" She noted something bulky in his pants pocket. Possibly a gun. She tried to remain calm. Calm had always been her friend. Calm never failed to save her.

"I followed you the other day."

Yeah, I got that, you psycho. She tightened her grip on the key inserted in the deadbolt while maintaining eye contact. Should she finish engaging the lock, or should she push on that door and attempt to get inside? No, she'd never make it; the man was standing too close.

"Why did you follow me?" She twisted her hand, yanked the key from the lock, and slid it into her shorts pocket.

"Because I knew you were going to rip me off. I just knew," he growled.

She took it the job hadn't been done on Saturday like he'd asked. But how was that her problem? She'd given the money to the guy with the scratchy voice. Not that this was any of her business.

Keep telling yourself that. She raised her hands, attempting to show Rick that she was no threat. *Get his guard down. Then run.* "I'm sorry. I only take messages. That's it." The snarl on his face told her he wasn't going to accept her excuse, so she added, "But the money is still sitting in the drawer. Mr. Sampson never came to pick it up." A partial lie.

"Why? Where is he?"

"I get paid to answer the phone. He doesn't involve me in his business. But if you want your money back, we can go to the office right now, and I'll give it to you." She couldn't tell him that she'd handed it over to some man who'd shown up and threatened her. He wouldn't be happy. Convincing Rick to go to the office only bought her a few minutes to think. Or run. Or...*something.*

"Got a car? We can go right now," she urged.

His brown eyes flickered with suspicion. He wasn't biting.

"I'm sorry, Rick," she added, hoping to sway

him, "but it's not like I have fifty thousand just sitting around to give you. Look where I live."

He bit the edge of his lower lip and chewed aggressively. She was getting through to him. "I want to talk to Sampson."

"Then call him. But if you think I've got some magic way to track him down or get him to answer, I don't. He calls *me* when he needs something," she lied. They'd only spoken the one time. Of course, the caller ID had been blocked, so she had no way of calling him back. The scratchy-voice man said he knew where Sampson lived, but it wasn't like she'd be calling him for help. Even if she had his number. Which she didn't.

Rick narrowed his shifty eyes. "Fine. We'll go to the office, but if you try anything, I'll kill you. Understand?"

Emily refrained from laughing. If she had a nickel for every time she'd heard those words, she'd be living on her own private island. "I understand."

He jerked his head in the direction of a dark green SUV parked along the edge of the chain-link fence separating the apartment complex from the liquor store next door.

She marched toward the vehicle, trying to stay calm. *Calm is my ally. Calm means survival.*

"Nice place, by the way." He kicked an empty beer can out of his way and then unlocked the passenger-side door for her.

He must've noticed the fancy decorative paper bags and discarded vodka fifths. They littered the patches of overgrown dried grass that had made homes along the base of the fence.

"Some see urban decay. I see motivation to work harder," she said, getting into the SUV.

"You're an odd one, aren't you?"

Says the man threatening to kill me. She shrugged, trying to mask the panic swimming in her stomach.

"Guess you'd have to be if you're working for Sampson." He slammed the door shut and came around to the driver's side, giving her a few seconds to firm up her plan. The street she lived on was a main thoroughfare that ran east to west through the south of town. There was a stoplight every few blocks, and at this time of day, traffic clogged every intersection. Most people turned and took shortcuts down the smaller side streets to avoid it. Whatever route he chose, he would have to stop or slow down. She would jump out at the first chance and run.

He would likely assume she'd come back here to her apartment to get her stuff, but she wouldn't. There was nothing she couldn't leave behind—a few toiletries from the dollar store, a frying pan and pot she'd picked up at the thrift store, along with her cheap work outfits. At best, it was a few hundred bucks' worth of items, including the free mattress and sheets she'd gotten from the church down the road that helped women in need. Still, it killed her to have to run again, but what choice did she have?

The guy slid inside the SUV and grabbed her hand. Before she could react, he'd handcuffed himself to her.

"What the…?" Her mouth fell open.

"In case you get any bright ideas."

Shit. Shit. Shit!

He cranked the engine and merged into traffic. Her mind spun frantically. If they made it back to that office, she was screwed.

She'd counted five opportunities she could have had to jump from the green SUV hurtling toward imminent doom. Five chances to save herself she'd never get. But they were already halfway to the office, and whining about hypotheticals wouldn't help her.

Think of something. Think! A story to convince him not to kill her or a weapon inside the office. But there was nothing in that shithole that could kill him unless he was game to wait around for a cup of coffee. Her best bet was making a move before they got to the strip mall. With him driving, she might be able to discreetly signal someone who would then call the police.

No. Bad idea. Cops might save her initially, but then they'd start asking questions. They might ask for her ID and notice that the Emily in the picture had a round face compared to her oval one. Also, their noses were nothing alike, hers being much perkier with a scar in the middle—a gift from Ed.

The only option? Talk to Rick and *keep* him talking. She was good at that—making conversation. It had been one of the few tools she possessed when Ed was in a mood, ready to take it out on her. Talking calmed him, made him focus on something else.

"So, um…how do you know Mr. Sampson?" she asked.

The man glanced sideways but remained focused on the busy traffic. "Same as any person."

"The want ads?"

He chuckled with a condescending edge. "Yeah, right."

"That's how I met him."

"The want ads?" More condescending chuckles.

"I'm serious. I answered an ad for a receptionist. I don't even know what he actually does."

Rick rubbed his sweaty brow with the back of his hand, forcing her arm to go with it. "Don't give a fuck. All I care about is getting my fifty thousand back."

Suddenly, she saw a window cracked open,

leading to salvation. "Yeah, but like you said, the job wasn't done. Why not wait a few more days? See if Mr. Sampson can make things right?"

His one hand tightened on the steering wheel. "You think I'm fucking around here? We're not talking about a pizza you mistakenly put pineapple on."

Don't say pizza. Her stomach rumbled. "Agreed. But I sense that whatever service Mr. Sampson provides is hard to come by."

"He's not on Yelp, that's for fucking sure."

"Then let me talk to Sampson—see what can be worked out."

"You said you had no way to contact him." Rick sounded cocky all of a sudden, like he'd caught her in a lie and that somehow made him a superior human being.

"Yes. *He* contacts *me*. And I'm sure he will."

They arrived to the dumpy strip mall. Rick pulled into the spot right in front of the frosted-glass door. She looked up at the thick black numbers painted above the doorway. "*Suite #45*" was starting to feel like a curse.

Rick unlocked his end of the handcuffs and produced the gun she suspected was there all along. "No bullshit or I shoot you. Got it?"

"Are you sure you don't want to wait for Mr. Samp—"

"I want my fucking money!" he yelled, his dark strands of hair falling in his face.

"Okay. Okay." She slowly exited the car, praying for a miracle. There had to be some way out of this. She bent down and lifted the doormat, but—

Where's the key? She spun in a circle. *Maybe when I threw it, it bounced or—*

"What are you doing?" Rick growled, standing beside her, the gun back in his pocket.

"The key's gone." She dropped the thick rubber mat.

He slapped her hard. "Stupid bitch! You left the key under the doormat, with my fifty thousand inside?"

She cupped her cheek and stared up at him, that feeling she knew all too well seeping into her brain. Cold, hard fear. It was the sort of fear that triggered a chain reaction. First, all emotion shut down. Screaming or crying when Ed hit her only made it worse. He expected her to take her punishment and do nothing to make him feel guilty about being such a violent man. One tear, one whimper, and he unleashed hell. He hated weakness—in himself and within others. Second, her body went numb. Sometimes, she'd wake the next morning with cuts that still bled. She never remembered Ed giving them to her, but he had.

"You'd better pray the money's still in there." Rick walked back to his SUV, reached under the seat, and produced a crowbar.

It was her chance to run. Maybe her only chance. There were plenty of cars passing on the street, so all she needed was for one person to stop.

She turned her body, preparing to bolt, just as the office door popped open. Standing inside the office, with arms crossed over his large chest and a gun with a silencer in his hand, was the scratchy-voiced man.

"And just who the hell are you?" he growled at Rick.

Rick's mouth flapped for a moment. "Are-are you Sampson?"

"No."

Rick dropped the crowbar and grabbed her from behind, putting his gun to her head. It happened so fast, Emily felt her teeth clack.

The exterminator guy didn't flinch. "You probably aren't aware," he said with an ominous tinge to his voice, "but there are rules in this line of work. For all the players, including clients. I'm assuming you're unfamiliar with them, so I'll give you three seconds to drop the gun, let her go, and leave."

She couldn't see Rick's face, but she suspected he was either pissing himself or debating his next move. Possibly both.

"One," said Mr. Cold Eyes. "Two."

"Hey, man. I just want my money back,"

stuttered Rick.

"Thr—"

Rick dropped his arm and scurried back to his SUV.

Emily rushed inside the office, away from Rick and toward Mr. Cold Eyes, and shut the door. She bent over for a moment to catch her breath. When she stood up straight again, the man with the scratchy voice looked at her and scowled.

"Your face," he said.

He had to be referring to the red welt on her cheek. "Compliments of Rick. At least he kept his hand open, though. A true gentleman." She pressed her palm over the spot. It didn't hurt, but the skin was hot. "I'll be okay. I've had worse." All that mattered was she was safe. For now, at least.

Mr. Cold Eyes remained silent on the matter. At least in the context of words. His body, on the other hand, was saying all sorts of things. The tendons flexed in his muscular arms, and a vein pulsed in his thick strong neck.

Rick's engine roared to life outside, and she could hear the vehicle pulling away.

"You wait here," Cold Eyes snarled. "I want to talk to you when I come back." He took the safety off his gun and charged out the door, slamming it shut behind him.

Emily suddenly heard noises—glass cracking and a grunt. Then she heard the SUV leaving.

After a few moments, Emily went to the door, cracked it open, and peeked outside at the parking lot. *What the...?*

Both men were gone.

CHAPTER FOUR

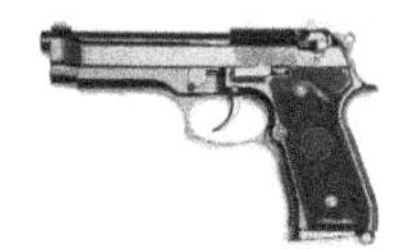

Emily stayed put at her desk all morning, shivering in her black running shorts and asking herself two questions: What were the consequences of staying? What were the consequences of leaving town?

There was no doubt in her mind that Rick was dead, because she knew perfectly well what kind of "rats" this "exterminator" man dealt with. *If it talks like a hit man, looks like a hit man, and walks like a hit man, it sure as hell isn't a duck.*

That was just the sort of thing her late father, Big Carl, would say if he were here now. He had been a simple man who loved his fishing boat and the sea, which was why her aunt Mary had raised her. Her dad would come ashore every few months for a weekend here or there, and when he did, every minute together felt magical. He would tell her stories of sea monsters and brave sailors.

He would make her laugh with ridiculous jokes about fish or whales. Then he'd leave, and she'd miss him all over again until the missing turned into the excitement of knowing he'd soon be home.

Then came the day she'd found out the missing would never stop.

She had been twelve when the ocean claimed her dad's life somewhere off the coast of Maine. The devastation nearly killed her. She couldn't eat, sleep, or stop crying. It was Aunt Mary who helped her through the grief: "Just picture your dad smiling up at the waves, his arms wide open as they took him home for good." It was no secret to anyone that the place he loved most in this world was on his boat. It was why Emily's mother left when she was little. Aunt Mary said that every time Dad went out to sea, her mother would spiral into a depression, unable to cope with being abandoned. As to how or why that would make her mother leave and do the very same thing to Emily, no one would ever know.

Luckily, Aunt Mary had been a great mother. *The best.* She was always there to help with homework and cheer her on in gymnastics. Aunt Mary taught her how to ride a bike and drive a car. Mary put blonde highlights in Emily's red hair and curled it for her first high school dance. The only part of her Emily hated was how she'd left. Cancer. Mary died five years after Big Carl, when Emily was just seventeen. A group home was the only option for those gruelingly sad six months until she'd reached eighteen and finished high school.

After that, the bad decisions started, and the life Emily once had, peppered with happy memories between the hard ones, ended.

Bad decision number one: moving to Atlantic City with two other girls who'd also just turned eighteen from the group home. It was a road that would eventually lead to Ed.

If only she had stopped to think, *really* think about her choices back then. If she had been patient and planned her moves, things would have played out differently. Of course, that was hindsight. The question was, could that thinking save her now?

Stay.

Or go.

Sitting at her desk, Emily nervously tapped the point of her pen on the pad of paper. Rick was no longer a threat, so that was a plus. On the other hand, the exterminator had told her to stay put. What did he want with her?

Maybe it was better to run and not find out, but she didn't have any money to start all over again. Of course she'd do it if there was no other option to protect herself, but if Mr. Cold Eyes had wanted to hurt her, he would've done it by now. *Or he would've let Rick take care of me.*

Instead, Cold Eyes had defended her and…

And I can't even think about it. Was another human being really dead because of her?

She heard a car pull up just outside the door. The exterminator was back.

She waited anxiously as footsteps approached outside, but when the door opened, it wasn't him.

A petite woman with dark hair, wearing sunglasses and a blue baseball cap, came inside. "Hi. Umm…I'm looking for Mr. Sampson? I made an appointment a couple of weeks ago."

"He's not here, but I can take a message." Emily noticed the woman's hands were shaking and there was a black eye hidden under those sunglasses. Emily's heart twisted in her chest.

"When will he be back?" The woman's voice cracked with worry.

"I'm really sorry; I don't know. But I promise to give him your message." Emily slid the pad of paper toward the woman and set the pencil down next to it.

The woman stared at the paper. "Um, it's just—I don't know when I can come back, and it's not safe for him to call me."

Emily pushed back her urge to tell the woman to run or fight or do anything other than return to the person who was hurting her. "If you're having a *pest* issue, I'm sure Sampson can help," she said, with a firm tone. "Just leave your message."

What am I doing? Why am I getting involved? She knew that Sampson was nowhere to be found, but she couldn't simply turn the woman away. Not when Emily knew all too well about her situation.

The lady bobbed her head nervously. "O-okay. Okay." She leaned over and started writing. "This is the address. Eight tonight is the only window for a while—I'll be at my mother's."

Tonight? Oh no... The chances of Sampson miraculously showing up today were probably zero—it was anyone's guess where he was. Or if he was still alive. *Well, someone was paying me.* On the other hand, there was such a thing as automatic payments. Bottom line, she just didn't know what was up with him.

The woman reached into her brown leather purse and handed Emily six bundles of cash. "Mr. Sampson said if I wanted it done quickly, I had to pay an extra ten."

Emily closed her hand around the thick stack. "I'll be sure the message is passed along."

"Thank you." The woman rushed out, nearly in tears.

Emily hissed out a breath. What was she going to do? Clearly this woman was terrified and needed help. She herself had been there so many times—the fear, the desperation—but she had never been brave enough to take action. Ed knew all the men who did "pest control" work in their city. Word would have gotten back to him if she'd gone that route. And, of course, she'd been too afraid to call the police on Ed, but that had more to do with the fact that Ed was an FBI agent and his brother was a cop. Both of them were as corrupt as hell, something she'd learned far too late into the marriage.

Emily listened for the car to leave, and slid the bundles in the drawer. She rapped her nails on the metal desk, the worry in the pit of her stomach spiraling. What if the job didn't get done because Sampson was nowhere to be found? She sure as hell hadn't seen the man, and it had been over one week since she'd started "working" here. Bottom line, if she left the money and the note in the desk drawer, they could sit there forever.

That poor woman. Emily's stomach churned harder as she thought about that lady coming home tonight, seeing the husband—boyfriend—whatever—standing there, ready for his routine. Maybe it was a liter of whisky first. Maybe he liked to go out and play poker all night, her fate resting on whether he won or lost.

Emily's heart pounded, the harsh memories triggering her panic. Suddenly, all she could think of was helping that woman. Nothing else mattered. And thankfully, the solution was straightforward: Emily was there to take and give messages, so that was exactly what she'd do.

As for the reason Mr. Cold Eyes wanted her to

stay? Who knew? She'd have to wing it and see what was what.

A short while later, heavy footsteps approached the door. In stepped Mr. Cold Eyes looking agitated—flat lips, tight unshaved jaw, menacing blaze in his eyes—like he was in no mood for bullshit.

"Oh. You're back," she said, putting on her calmest face. She was not about to mention Rick or ask what happened. She could guess. What she didn't know was why he'd decided to kill Rick, but it was the sort of question she didn't want an answer to. What if Rick had just rubbed him the wrong way? What if he didn't like the fact that Rick saw his face? "By the way, you just missed Mr. Sampson. He left a message for you."

Mr. Cold Eyes lifted a dark brow, those unnerving gray orbs sharply focused on her.

"What?" she said defensively, hiding the fact that when he looked at her like that, her bladder quivered.

"Sampson was here? Just now?"

"Yes."

"Why isn't he answering his phone?" he asked.

She shrugged. "Not sure. He just mentioned something about having to lie low. Said he'd check in or call in a few days."

The man let out a low growl and ran his hand through his dark short mane. "Son of a bitch.

Probably started messing around with Rose again," he muttered.

"Who's Rose?"

He gave her a look. "Didn't Sampson tell you the rule about questions?"

"Yes. And you just broke it. Several times, in fact." She stared up at him defiantly, wanting to show him she wasn't going to be talked down to, that she was part of this team. Sampson, after all, had hired her. "Here's the address of the infestation. Eight o'clock is ideal since the customer will be out of the house." She pulled the cash bundles from the drawer, slapped them on the desk, and pushed them forward.

"I'm already booked." He didn't bother looking at the money.

Dammit. Sampson would have known this guy's schedule and taken that into consideration. "Sampson said to make it work. There's an inconvenience fee included, of course."

The man stared at her for a moment, sending a wave of shivers down her spine. "All right. But I get an extra ten for the other job he already booked me on."

"Another ten," she repeated, her throat tight. Where would she come up with another ten? "If that's the deal you have with Sampson…" She shrugged, as if she couldn't give a damn because it had nothing to do with her. Of course, that wasn't true. "Was that all? You'd said you wanted to discuss something right before you left."

"Yeah," he said, "I wanted you to pass another message to Sampson. Tell him client forty-three went smoothly—no more rats—but I guess he already knew that since the money is here waiting. I'll be back in the morning for my hundred and twenty, so don't be late. I've got those jobs in Chicago, and my flight leaves at noon tomorrow." He grabbed the cash.

Wait. What? Hundred and twenty? Emily sat frozen, trying to figure out why the man wanted so much money.

Oh shit. Oh shit. It suddenly dawned on her; he only got paid *after* the job was done. He thought the money she'd just handed him was for a job he did last night. Tomorrow, he would want to be paid for two more jobs. *Plus overtime.* How was she going to come up with that much cash?

At least that woman would have her pest-control issue taken care of.

Yeah, then I'll be next on the pest list.

"Sure. Got it. I'll pass on the message," she said confidently.

Mr. Cold Eyes turned those wide shoulders and went for the door, stopping just shy of it. "Oh, and by the way, you dropped the key outside." He pulled something from his jeans pocket and tossed it toward her. The key landed with a clank directly in front of her on the desk. "I'd be careful not to lose it because you sure as hell won't be getting inside here without it."

She stared blankly, having no clue what he meant.

"Didn't Sampson mention that this place is like Fort Knox?"

This dump looked like it couldn't keep a fart safe. "No. He didn't."

"The door and windows are made with tempered security glass." He jerked his head toward the AC unit. "And I wouldn't mess with that if I were you. Not unless you want ten thousand volts of electricity running through you."

She glanced at the unit grinding away. *It's a booby trap?* "But who would want to break in here? There's nothing to steal."

He lifted a brow. "See you tomorrow morning."

Why hadn't Sampson warned her the unit was rigged? *Well, that explains why it's hardwired to run nonstop.* What it didn't explain was why this place was fortified.

Maybe there's something inside the cabinets? She got up and poked the one on the right with her finger. Who knew what else might be rigged?

Nothing happened, so she went in for a bold knock. A hollow echo answered back. It sounded empty. She moved to the cabinet in the middle, jarring it against the wall. Nothing rattled, and it felt fairly light.

She stood there for a moment, trying to figure

out what was so dang valuable in this office. Not that she intended to steal anything; snooping was just her thing. It also proved useful from time to time. It was how she'd learned the details of what Ed really did for a living.

Staring at the cabinets, she noticed something crawl up from behind them. "Eww…" Another roach. She took her running shoe off and smashed the thing.

"Wait." *That sounded weird.* She rapped her knuckles against the bubbling yellow wallpaper. The wall produced a faint vibration, almost as if there was some sort of thick metal underneath, not sheetrock. Curious to test another wall, she put her shoe back on and walked over to that god-awful coffee pot on the other side of the room.

She knocked on the wall behind it. *Hollow.* Like regular sheetrock. She looked over her shoulder, eyeing the space behind the filing cabinets where the dead roach sat immortalized, one with the wallpaper. Her guess was that if this office had something to protect, it was behind that wall. Maybe a safe room?

She started looking around the office for a way in—a lever, button, or remote under her desk, under her chair, under the sink. She looked up at the water-stained ceiling made up of those industrial panels with little holes. The one over by the counter was slightly askew.

She tested the yellow Formica with her

weight. It seemed sturdy enough. She climbed up, being careful not to knock the Mr. Coffee to the floor.

She cautiously poked the ceiling tile, wondering what might happen. *Nothing.* She gave it another poke.

Suddenly, a big spider skittered out and dropped on her face.

"Gah!" She swiped it away and turned to hop down, her foot clipping the coffee carafe. The thing crashed to the floor, glass going everywhere.

A metal key lay right there amongst the shards.

Interesting. She hopped off the counter, being cautious to avoid the glass with her fingers. Emily held up the key and inspected it closely. Honestly, it looked like a regular old house key.

She pivoted around the room, searching for a place to use it. *Well, we know the AC unit isn't it.* She did another lap around the room. There were no other locks aside from the one in the front door. *And the filing cabinets.* She glanced over at the three metal boxes. The one in the middle had a lock that looked worn. The ones on the edges looked like they'd never been touched.

No. That would be way too easy. She walked over to try it out anyway. She slid the key inside the cabinet's lock and heard a pop to her left.

Just beside the cabinets, a little panel in the wall swung inward.

Seriously? She tiptoed over and pushed the door, keeping her body a few feet from whatever was inside the dark space. *Probably a roach garden or spider amusement park.* But she couldn't see anything.

She went for her purse, grabbed her phone, and turned on the flashlight function. She held it out in front of her and returned to the opening in the wall, pushing carefully on the wallpapered panel. Still, she couldn't see a thing.

Cautiously, she stepped closer and poked her head inside. There was a glowing light switch on the right. She flipped it on and gasped.

CHAPTER FIVE

Abandoned strip mall, my ass. She had never seen anything like this except maybe in the movies. (And not the nice ones about nice people.) This was straight out of a hardcore narco flick, minus the bricks of cocaine.

The first room, which was made of cinderblock walls and concrete floors, contained over a hundred guns—rifles, handguns, and all the other stuff she didn't know how to use. Her husband had only owned "standard issue" FBI revolvers, which, she'd learned, weren't so standard issue after all. Ed had had to file a special request to carry one. Why a revolver? She'd once heard him and his gang of vile, rapey bastards talking about how only a "dumb motherfucker who wanted to get caught" would use anything else.

Bottom line: Evidence was the devil. A revolver kept the casings inside until the shooter ejected them, preferably at a time and place of their choosing. Those other handguns with the magazines spit the casings out, and if one was in a hurry, it was a little difficult to pick them up.

Her eyes glided over the rows and rows of guns hung along the cinder-block wall, like tiny soldiers waiting to be called into action.

God, I hate guns. They reminded her of everything violent in the world.

She cautiously continued through the room, noting a few boxes and crates with more guns stacked neatly in the corner. Was Sampson preparing for Armageddon?

She opened the heavy steel door leading to the next room, which, if her calculations were correct, would place her somewhere behind the walls of the vacant dry cleaning business next door. It seemed like the strip mall, which was a long rectangular building divided into six individual business spaces, was also divided down its length. Six shops on one side faced the street, and hidden rooms on the back side of the building. This layout was pretty ingenious, actually.

She flipped on the light in the next room to find several monitors sitting on a desk piled up with newspapers. No laptop or computers, though. Sampson probably had those locked away. On the other side of the room were open-faced shelving units filled with manila folders like she'd seen at her dentist's office.

She walked over and plucked out a folder. It had a number on the upper right-hand corner. This one in particular was "#68." She opened the folder and thumbed through the handwritten notes.

"What in the…?"

Client: 68
Job: Reverend Thomas Moore.
Verified: 3 victims. Ages 8, 11 and 12.
Females.
Fee: $80,000
Assigned to Operator: 18

The notes went on to describe Moore's daily routine—which stores he liked to frequent, how he liked to go to the gym across the street from a daycare facility, and when he was most likely to be at home.

So Sampson researches people first. The rest of the file contained photos, news articles, a police report and a copy of a court proceeding. Emily's eyes scanned the tiny print for details, noting that Mr. Moore's court case had been dismissed. On the last page was a form that looked to have been filled out by Sampson.

Closed: April 8, 2015
Completed by Operator: 18
Payout: $50,000
Bonus: N

She placed the file back in its spot and grabbed another. Number three-ninety-four. This one was for a man named Rodrigo Hernandez.

"Verified eighty-four murders? Jesus, was he a serial killer?"

But no. Emily went on to read that he was a member of one of three cartels in Northern Mexico who apparently lived on this side of the border. There was a list of addresses, the names of his victims, the number of people living in his house, including the maid and girlfriend.

Fee: $2,000,000
Assigned to Operator: 12

She flipped to the back page, noting the payout was two hundred thousand dollars, completed by operator twelve. She also noted there were discrepancies between the fee the client paid and what the operator received. Did Sampson keep the difference for himself? For business expenses? Both?

She reviewed several more files, finding a governor—who'd murdered some man's wife—another drug dealer, and a CEO of some chemical company who was dumping military-grade toxic waste into a river that was the only source of water for a Native American tribe in Utah. Over fifty documented deaths.

Wow. Who the hell was this Sampson guy?

Because this operation did not seem like your average group of criminals looking to make a few bucks. Specifically, four things jumped out at her in these files: (1) Only the target's identity was revealed. The payer, or client, was never mentioned, nor was the operator's name. She guessed this information was kept somewhere safe. (2) Mr. Sampson appeared to only take jobs for people who were not so nice. In fact, he seemed to take great care in verifying the targets' misdeeds along with collecting key information for the operator. (3) Sampson was keeping a lot of freaking money for himself. (4) The man she'd met with the gray eyes wasn't the only operator.

How many were there? Where did they live? How did Sampson get ahold of them? These were all questions of curiosity more than anything. Because this was some very serious, very scary shit.

Emily set the file back in its place and whooshed out a breath, scrubbing her face with her hands. She strongly suspected that Sampson was dead. Considering the level of organization and attention to detail in these files, it seemed out of place that Rick's job never got done over the weekend and that Sampson missed a payment to Mr. Cold Eyes. That was where the mix-up happened. When she'd handed Rick's cash to Cold Eyes, Cold Eyes thought he was getting paid for some other job he'd completed. He'd had no clue the money was from another client for another job. Rick's job.

Anyway, Sampson had dropped the ball at least twice now. Three times if she counted the woman from today. Given the life-or-death stakes of this business, it didn't seem probable Sampson would just leave without putting anyone at the helm. Not that she knew the man, but the odds didn't look good for Sampson. As her dad used to say, *"Even beekeepers get stung."* It meant that despite being experts in bees and wearing protective gear, the fact was they surrounded themselves with stinging insects. And, no matter how good they were at their jobs, people made mistakes. The natural consequence of making a mistake as a beekeeper is getting stung.

The natural consequence of managing a group of hit men is that you'll get hit.

What she couldn't understand, though, was why hire her? This seemed like the type of business that required a high level of secrecy and trust. *Didn't take me long to figure out what they really do.* So why bring in a stranger, knowing she'd find out? It wasn't as if Sampson had had a lot of time to research her and know for certain she wouldn't blab. She had seen his ad in the local paper: *Wanted: Receptionist to answer phone. Must be trustworthy. We pay cash.* She'd called the number, which sent her to some Google Voice account, like the one she had, since she didn't dare give out her new burner cell number to anyone—too easy to trace. Then she'd left her name, number, and email address per the instructions in the ad.

Sampson emailed her two hours later and then called for the "interview" that evening. She supposed he could have done a quick search on her name, but there were hundreds of Emily Rockfords in the US.

Anyway, that interview turned out to be a series of short questions—*"Do you do drugs or have a drinking problem? Have you ever been fired from a job? Are you able to write legibly?"*

No, no, and yes, she'd replied. He then said he'd try her out and see how things went. She said okay. He gave her the instructions regarding where to go and what to do. No fanfare. No application to sign. No request for her social.

He probably planned to kill me if things didn't work out.

A shiver crept up her spine. These were very dangerous people. Her only option now was to leave this city and never look back. The problem was making sure Mr. Cold Eyes didn't come after her, looking for his payout. He would likely assume she took the money and ran.

If only I could pay him before I leave. Then he wouldn't follow. Hell, maybe I could even stay in El Paso.

Sampson had to keep money around to run his business. Right? It was probably in a safe, along with the lists of names—clients and operators. She spun around in the center of the room. There were at least four other sections to this strip mall. Six retail spaces total.

Her eyes caught the slight indentation—a long vertical groove—in the wall exactly where another door should be. She walked over and was about to touch it when she felt the hairs on her arm stand straight up. She pulled back her hand.

What is that? She brought her hand close to the wall again. The fine reddish-blond hairs lifted from her skin. *Static.* She leaned in a little closer and listened, detecting a faint buzzing sound inside. It reminded her of those power lines by Aunt Mary's old house. On a windy day they sounded like a swarm of insects.

Whatever was on the other side of that wall, she suspected it was booby-trapped like the AC, which meant it was something Sampson wanted to protect. Money? Files? His computers? All of the above? Either way, she wasn't about to end up like a toasted marshmallow.

She flipped off the lights, placed the cabinet key under the coffee maker, went to her desk, and wrote out a brief note saying that she was sorry. She'd only been trying to help that woman.

Would Mr. Cold Eyes even care about the reason for not getting paid? *Fat chance.* The guy killed people. For money. It was highly unlikely he'd wake up tomorrow and say, "Yanno what?

This getting-paid part of my murder job is getting old. I should just do it for free."

Which was why she signed off her note:

I don't know where Sampson is. I have no money. Don't bother looking for me because you won't find me. — Jane

That last part was a hope more than a statement, of course.

She placed the note on the desk before heading out.

This time, she really meant it. She would not be coming back. Not for anything.

That night, Emily did some quick research on her phone to prepare for her departure to Yuma, Arizona, her "plan B" location right on the Mexican border. Her mind kept drifting back to those hidden rooms inside suite forty-five. She had grown to like puzzles over the last few years. Or perhaps it had just been more of a habit, cultivated by the need to survive. Being around Ed and his crew had taught her to keep her mouth shut and listen carefully. They always spoke in codes, thinking they were clever, but it never took long to figure out what they were really up to. In short, her secret hobby had taught her a lot about how they operated and what kind of people they were. It had also led her to the terrifying, horrible truth about Ed's side business.

Ed will pay. The day was coming. She'd make sure of it.

Back to the rooms, though. The thing she was learning about Sampson was that he liked puzzles, too. The strip mall was a puzzle made of rooms. The office was a puzzle with keys and traps to keep his secrets safe. His business was structured like a puzzle with numbers and codes. *Honestly, it's like Sampson's daring me to figure out where his money is.*

If she did that, she could pay Mr. Cold Eyes, and with the debt paid, maybe he would leave her alone. Then she could stay in town and focus on what she really wanted: working on her plan for Ed. Moving, finding work, and saving money for another new ID—if she could even get one— would set her back months.

So was it worth it to go back to that office and look one more time? Again, it wasn't like she planned to rob Mr. Sampson. She merely wanted to make things right and pay Cold Eyes.

Her duffel bag already packed and sitting on the bed, she decided to take it with her. If she couldn't crack the puzzle to get into that other secret room, she'd head straight to the bus station and keep going all the way to Yuma.

CHAPTER SIX

Just past nine p.m., the Uber driver dropped her off three blocks from the office, at a dive bar with a flashing neon sign of a naked woman kicking her legs to the sides. She wondered what sort of clientele it attracted because, to her, it looked like a warning: *Get your hot gonorrhea here! Fiery STDs for ya!*

Uh. No thanks.

Dressed in her travel clothes—a plain white tee, blue hoodie, jeans, and black Converse—she waited until the driver was gone before hoofing it to the suite. Just didn't feel right letting him know where she was really going. Truth was, she felt a little guilty going to look for money that didn't belong to her.

She went into the gas station across the street to grab a Red Bull, taking a few extra moments to peruse the magazines near the plate-glass window at the front. From there, she had a view of the entrance to the office. Though it was fairly dark over there, she didn't see anything—lights, movement, cars, or people.

Well, here goes. She paid for her drink, chugged it outside, threw the can in the recycle bin, and dashed across the street, with her duffel bag slung over her shoulder.

The entire front of the strip mall was quiet save for the passing trucks on the street behind her. She bent down, found the key right where she'd left it—thank God—and slipped inside the office, only using the light of her cell to look for the second key.

Wonderful. This place is even creepier at night. The glass from the broken carafe crunched beneath her tennis shoes as she made her way to the counter. She would've cleaned up the mess, but with what? Mr. Sampson didn't even have a Kleenex in this place. Just lots of guns.

She grabbed the key from under the Mr. Coffee and opened the panel leading to the first hidden room. Once inside, she closed the door and flipped on the lights.

The room lit up with blinding fluorescents. After her eyes adjusted, she set down her bag on the concrete floor and took in the space. Mr. Sampson liked to hide his keys. Why? Maybe he was old school. Maybe he knew how easy it was for things like fingerprint scanners or number pads to get hacked. Basically, anything with a chip could be messed with—according to Ed's thugs. A key, on the other hand, was simple. You had it or you didn't. Keys could be hidden anywhere. *Right under a person's nose, for example.*

"No way would he make it that easy." She walked past the files to the electrified wall and inspected the floor. Nothing.

She pulled a rubber band from her pocket, tied back her hair, and got on her hands and knees to take a closer look. A few loose strands of brown hair flopped in her face, reminding her she was way overdue to dye her red roots. She couldn't alter her body type (unless she hit the lotto so she could eat nonstop or get plastic surgery), she couldn't change her five-five height or wear annoying contacts to modify her green eyes, but her hair was something she *could* transform. And it gave her a drastically different look. More serious. More grown up. The red always made her feel self-conscious. People expected her to be a fiery, brave, wild woman—an image she could never live up to, even when she wanted.

Maybe it's time to rethink that. But how, exactly, did one go about changing themselves on the inside? She wished she knew, because she would give anything to stop feeling so afraid all the time.

Emily tucked away her fallen locks and ran her fingertips over the floor. She didn't see anything. No cracks. No seams in the concrete.

She stood, tilted back her head, and examined the ceiling. It was made of smooth white stucco. No edges. No ripples. Nowhere to hide a key.

She pivoted, doing a three-sixty. *Where would I hide a key?* Maybe in one of the folders? Under K for key?

K was the—she counted on her fingers—eleventh letter in the alphabet.

She shrugged. Wouldn't hurt to look. She quickly sorted through the file cubbies and found folder number eleven. She pulled it out and—

The contents spilled to the floor. There was a photo of what used to be a woman. Bound. Gagged. Very bad things done to her bloody face. Emily's stomach rolled. Who had done that to her? It almost made her grateful that people like Sampson existed.

Not wanting to see the gruesome image again, she looked away and used her fingers to feel for the photo, sliding it back into the folder facedown. If she never ever saw anything that horrific and gory for the rest of her life, it would be too soon. She just hoped that the person responsible had been dealt with.

Emily quickly thumbed through the remaining contents of the folder, noting that the last page said:

Closed: November 2, 2009

Operator: 1

Good. The asshole who did it was dead, compliments of operator number one. She would bet her only pair of PJs that was Sampson's number. He was the boss.

I wonder how he got all this started. People, in her opinion, did not get into these shady lines of work by plan or by choice. They stumbled into it or were pushed. Her husband, for example, had been lured in by his brother, his brother by an uncle. But it didn't really matter *who* got them started, because it worked the same for everyone. It began with an insider asking for "a favor." Generally, an illegal favor. "Hey, Joe. I need someone to pick up my lost suitcase from the airport. They finally found it and called. Can you help me out?" From there, the group owned their asses. "You do what I say, Joe, or I'll be sure the DA finds a nice video of you carrying that suitcase full of heroin." One favor, one misstep suddenly turned into another errand, then another, ending in a lifetime of servitude, with each crime getting bigger. The money that eventually came with these errands took the sting off. Ed, for example, bought a boat. His uncle owned a villa in Florida. Sugar-coated bitter pills. Maybe some in their group eventually acquired a taste for it, like a junky addicted to being bad. The point was, she suspected that a person had to fall into this line of work. Sampson likely started the same way. He'd had a bone to pick with someone, or maybe a friend asked him to help right a wrong. Who knew? But, from looking at the dates on these files, this was a business he'd been growing over time.

Her question was: Why kill instead of sending the targets to jail? None of them looked like nice people, and if Sampson was able to scrape up enough evidence to satisfy his own moral compass, then why not hand it over to the police?

An image of her dirty-cop brother-in-law popped into her head. *Never mind.* Cops like him were the exception, but she could understand why Sampson's customers might not want to risk these people getting away.

She sighed and placed the file back. Her hunch had been wrong about that hiding spot for the key, but she knew, given enough time, she would crack this. Unfortunately, the last bus for Yuma was leaving in an hour, and waiting until morning for another bus was not a smart choice. By then, Mr. Cold Eyes would be looking for his hundred-and-twenty-thousand-dollar payout.

She dug around the room some more, checking under every surface—desk, computer monitors, file cubbies. Whatever was in that protected room had to be important because Mr. Sampson hadn't made it so easy this time.

Speaking of time...

She looked at the clock on her phone. She had to go. Even if she didn't want to run again, there was no way to stay.

She grabbed her bag and froze. Something urged her to keep trying.

No. It's time to leave. Be smart! She drew in a steady breath, reminding herself that if she ended up dead in El Paso, her plans for Ed would never come to fruition. There would be no one to stop him.

Think about the women. Think.

Because that was the cold hard truth, wasn't it? None of this was really about her—she'd given up on life long ago. It was those poor women who'd given her the strength to finally leave Ed when she'd stood on her porch back in Jersey, nearly pissing herself as she thought about the consequences of defying her husband. She had to be strong. *For them.*

Emily turned to leave just as a phone rang. High-pitched. Loud. Not in the other room. She looked around and discovered another phone buried beneath those neatly folded newspapers on the desk with the monitors.

Wait. What am I doing? Don't answer it. Just keep walking. Every time she had contact with a person tied to this damned place, she ended up in a bigger mess.

The phone continued blaring like an alarm in her head. But what if it was Sampson? She could tell him what happened. She could ask him to pay his guy. If it wasn't Sampson, she'd simply hang up. Easy.

She stepped forward, grabbed the receiver and pressed it to her ear. "Hello?"

"Jane. Fucking hell, Jane," the deep, scratchy voice whispered.

It was Mr. Cold Eyes.

"They have me cornered," he panted.

"What?" Her blood thinned. "Who?"

"It's a fucking trap. Didn't Sampson vet the job you gave me today?" The desperation in his voice was palpable.

The guilt inside her spiraled, sending heat to her face. *She* set up this job. She, the woman who had no business setting up jack shit. "Um-um-I don't know. Where are you?"

"Where the fuck do you think?" he spat, keeping his voice low.

Sonofabitch. She vaguely remembered the address—Lasso Lane or something. "Okay. Okay. What do I do?"

"Follow the goddamned protocol, woman."

The protocol? I don't know any protocols! "Sampson never told me what that is." Her voice came out frantic and shaky.

"Then fucking call Sampson," he snarled.

That was the one thing she couldn't do. "He's not answering. I-I just tried him," she lied, hoping Mr. Cold Eyes would give her another solution.

Sadly, he did.

"Then alert the other operators. Some of them have to be in the—"

"In the what? In the what?" Emily pushed, but the line went dead.

She stared blankly at the wall in front of her. There was no one to call. No Sampson. No operators. She had nothing. And it was all her goddamned fault because *she'd* sent him on that job.

I'll call the police. She pushed the button on the phone to get a dial tone, but her finger hovered impotently over the nine. Would Mr. Cold Eyes really want the police showing up when he was in the middle of a hit gone wrong?

"God! Dammit!" She stomped her foot. "Why!" Why the fuck couldn't she just get out of this fucking town, out of this fucking mess!

She tilted back her head and exhaled slowly, grasping at the last wisps of sanity swirling in her head. She couldn't let Mr. Cold Eyes die. He'd stopped Rick from hurting her. He'd made sure Rick would never touch her again. And after being invisible for so many years, no one giving a shit if she lived or died, that meant something. Pathetic, but true.

She stared down at her black Converse, that Ping-Pong ball in her head going back and forth. Stay. Go. Stay. Go.

Go. The smart thing was to leave and never

look back. *But do I want to be smart, or do I want to be brave for once in my life?* She was tired of living under the heel of fear. She wanted to be strong and good and everything Ed was not.

"Fuck it." She marched into the next room, grabbed the only revolver she saw, checked to make sure it was loaded, and marched out the front door, locking it behind her.

CHAPTER SEVEN

And look at me Ubering to a gunfight. What could possibly go wrong with this plan? Emily directed the driver to drop her at the corner of Lasso Lane. It was dark out, but she could easily see the neighborhood was made up of your typical middle-class tract homes. Stucco, beige, cookie-cutter construction. Neat front yards. Flowers on mailboxes. They reminded her of the house she used to live in with Ed, but theirs had been in a gated community. Kind of ironic, since the gate was meant to keep out people like him. Criminals.

She thanked the driver and hopped out with the gun tucked into the back of her jeans, underneath her hoodie. A dog barked off in the distance, and a pizza-delivery guy drove by.

Now what? She couldn't remember the house number for the job, so she wasn't sure where Mr. Cold Eyes was holed up. Even if she found the place, how did one go about rescuing a hit man? How many people had him cornered?

Okay. Think. Think. He'd likely got to the job site, went inside to "take care of the rat," then realized something was off. *No rat, maybe?* Then he'd probably tried to make an exit and found someone, or someones, waiting outside to ambush him.

It made sense, right? If he'd already gotten out, then Mr. Cold Eyes would be on the run, not hunkered down calling for backup.

First things first. *Figure out which house he's in.* From there, she'd have to wing it.

Let's do this. She removed her hoodie and tied it around her waist. She took out her ponytail and put her hair up in a sloppy bun on top of her head. She got out her phone, pressed it to her ear, and started walking. "Oh, hi, Mom!" she said loudly, starting a fake gab about some shopping trip, filling the conversation with lots of "Oh wow" and "No. Seriously?"

Yep. I'm just a regular woman, out for my evening cardio, chattin' with my mother. Don't mind me, hit man's hit men.

According to the map on her phone, which she'd studied on the way here, Lasso Lane was about three blocks long, ending at the cross street up ahead. Sooner or later, she'd have to walk by the right house. Mr. Gray Eyes might hear her voice and signal to her or—

Or I will see a car with two sketchy dudes parked right out front of that house with no lights on. Like those guys right there. Her heart pounded furiously as she approached. *What do I do? What do I do?* There were likely more guys around back, waiting for Mr. Cold Eyes to come out, right? He'd said he was cornered.

I should shoot them. That's what I should do.

No. That sounded horrible. She could never just walk up to a person and pull the trigger in cold blood, not even knowing if they were armed. *What do I do?*

Time was up. The men spotted her but weren't making any moves. In fact, they seemed like the ones worried about looking suspicious, putting on a show, waving their hands and discussing something. Just two dudes sitting in a car, having a private chat.

She stopped five feet shy of the car, pretending to be engrossed in her phone conversation. "What! Mom! No! Don't do it!" she yelled into her phone. "Don't you dare go back to that man!" She started fake bawling. "No. No, Mom."

From the corner of her eye, she saw the men watching her.

"No! No! You will not go back to him, Mom! He's a bad guy!"

The hysterical yelling was beginning to get the attention of the neighbors. Lights were coming on in a few more driveways. Curtains moved as people looked out their windows. But, dammit, the men were still parked there.

Jesus. Do something.

There was only one stupid idea that came to mind.

She crossed to the middle of the street, stopped, and then yelled, "Oh, God. I think I'm having a heart attack! Someone call an ambulance." She fell down in the street.

A man came running out to help. Then a woman.

The blue car drove off.

After a thorough and very nerve-racking once-over from the paramedics, where she prayed they wouldn't notice the concealed weapon in the back of her jeans beneath the hoodie tied around her waist, they assured her that her breathing was normal and her heart rate was stable. Their prognosis for the fake affliction? They said she'd likely had a panic attack.

"Must've been that conversation with my mother," she'd said. "Can you believe her? Getting back with Leonard? He smokes around her, and he knows she has asthma! He's a gambling addict, and he cheats on her every chance he gets."

Surprisingly, everyone bought her little ruse,

and she went on her way, refusing the ride to the hospital. No need for that since she'd miraculously recovered.

Emily thanked the paramedics, silently noting that while they had not saved her life, their presence had saved someone else's.

After that, she grabbed an Uber, but as the car headed toward the office, she started having second thoughts. Did she really want to go back there? Her duffel bag was in the office, but those were all things she could ditch. On her person, she had her bank card, a little cash, and a driver's license. And a gun with a huge barrel shoved uncomfortably down her butt crack. *Now I really hate guns.*

She could get a cheap motel room, lie low for a few days, then catch a bus out of town. Maybe she could pay one of those "birds" to fly her away unnoticed.

Or I could go back to the office, grab my stuff, and leave the gun. The last thing she wanted was to carry a loaded weapon. Dumping it for someone else to find seemed unsafe too.

As the car neared the office, her mind went back into Ping-Pong mode. Stay. Go. Stay. Go. But she needed to be honest with herself; the real reason she wanted to go back didn't have anything to do with the gun or her stuff. She wanted to find out if Mr. Cold Eyes had made his escape during the ambulance commotion.

Maybe she'd go back, write a second note for him, and tell him to leave a message on her Google Voice number. *That's what I'll do.* Then off she'd go, away from El Paso, these hit men, and all the shade keeping her from her real purpose.

Once again, Emily directed the driver to drop her off a few blocks away. She hopped out and started walking toward the gas station across the street, but as she passed the side alley, she heard a *psst!*

She turned her head and noticed the tall, hulking shadow back near the dumpster.

Mr. Cold Eyes?

"Get the fuck off the street, you fucking idiot," he growled.

Definitely Cold Eyes. She glanced over her shoulder to see if anyone was watching. Silly, because cars and trucks were zooming by in both directions on the busy street leading to the border crossing. Lots of eyes. And it was anyone's guess if they were friend or foe.

As she approached, she noticed he was dressed in all black, including his baseball cap. A dark-colored duffel bag sat at his feet.

"What the fuck do you think you're doing?" He grabbed her and slammed her back to the brick wall.

"*Ooph!*" He didn't knock the air from her lungs, but it didn't feel so great. "Let go, asshole."

She grunted, trying to jerk her shoulders free.

"What the fuck happened back there?" he asked, completely unfazed by her efforts, maintaining his tight grip. He was strong. She was not. And she knew if she said the wrong thing, she would be found the next morning in that dumpster a few feet away.

"I saved your life. That's what," she snapped.

"Not that. Who the hell vetted the job?"

So an ass-saving means nothing, huh? It had to her. Otherwise, he wouldn't be standing here. "All I know is a woman came in, said she was there to meet Sampson. I told her he wasn't there, but I'd take a message. So that's what I did."

"So then what, you just handed the message off to me? Those were men from a drug cartel!" He grabbed the front of her T-shirt and slammed her against the wall again.

Fucker! Emily felt the fight building inside but once again found herself repeating the old pitiful patterns etched deeply into her survival brain.

She raised her palms, every inch of elevation burning her pride. "I didn't know there was a vetting process, and the woman seemed desperate. Her face was all beat up. I had to help!"

He dropped his hands from the front of her shirt, and just like that, his rage turned to frustration. The air between them cooled. "She was probably one of their junkies. You couldn't have known it was a setup." He looked away, his gaze fixing toward the busy street at the end of the narrow alley.

She said nothing because the truth was, she'd screwed up. She'd played in a sandbox that didn't belong to her. Hell, she didn't have a plastic shovel or a tiny bucket—sandbox basics.

"What happens now?" she asked quietly. The truce felt fragile, like she could shatter it with one misplaced word.

"We clean up."

"I'm no-not sure what that means."

"Those men," he pointed off toward the street, "work for one of three cartels who've been trying to get rid of us."

"Why?"

"Because there are rules, and they don't like following them."

Rules? It was the second time he'd mentioned that. The first time was with Rick. The good news was, Mr. Cold Eyes wasn't going to be asking for his hundred and twenty thousand dollars.

You so sure about that? she asked herself.

With a renewed saltiness, he turned his frustrations back to her. "You need to get ahold of Sampson and tell him it's time to move."

"Move? Where?" she asked.

"That's his problem."

This might be a good time to come clean. She'd let things go too far, and she was way, way out of her depth. "I'm sorry to tell you this, but

Sampson hasn't been checking in."

"I figured as much."

Why didn't he seemed surprised? "Does this happen a lot?"

"No."

She stared up at his unshaved face, the shadows casting dramatic angles off the hard planes of his high cheekbones and masculine brow.

He added, "People disappear in our line of business. Hazard of the trade."

"You think he's dead?"

He shrugged, like it didn't matter one way or another.

"But doesn't that make things kind of *over?*" she asked.

"Over?" He chuckled bitterly.

"Sorry. But I'm new to the, uh, pest-control world. If the boss is gone, how doesn't that put a wrench in things?"

"I never said it didn't, but this work never ends."

She sensed a deeper meaning there; however, none of this was her problem. "Whatever. Fine. It's over for me," she said. "I quit."

"Jane, maybe Sampson left that part of the job description out, but you've been misinformed about your options. There is no *out*. There is no *quitting.*"

"Sorry?"

"You know too much, and once you're in,

you're in."

The rage percolated inside her, but unlike the other times, this rage bubbled to the surface. "Like hell I'm in." She gritted her teeth.

He stared, completely silent. The unblinking look on his shadowy face told her he wasn't fucking around.

But why was there no out? She had been hired to answer the goddamned phones! That was it.

She stomped her foot—the only option to prevent her from punching him or breaking her knuckles on the brick wall. "No. No fucking way." She shook a finger at him. "I did not risk my life running from the psycho-frying-pan just to jump into the hit-man-fire."

"Keep your voice down."

"No," she hissed, "I will not be quiet. And I'm done being told what to do by angry, mean, fucked-up men with guns. I'm done. Done!"

Where this sudden surge of bravery came from, she didn't know, but one thing was crystal clear: The tectonic plate beneath her feet was crumbling.

Not in a good way.

In a very, *very* bad way.

She had been running on fumes to keep her head on straight, and now the stress of the past few years—the beatings, the threats, the rage— was finally catching up. The lid holding it all in was coming unscrewed. Yes, now of all moments.

In the back alley of a nasty-ass gas station in the worst part of town, while facing a man who ended people's lives for a living. Here, in this moment, was where she reached the end of her tattered rope. There was nowhere lower to sink. There was no more space inside her heart to hold it all in. She'd been robbed of everything—her self-worth, her real name, her freedom. She'd lost it all, and on top of that, she would never feel safe again. She would never trust again. Add all that together, and she knew there would never be peace in her heart. No happiness. Just revenge.

"Answer honestly, Jane. Have you ever met Sampson?" he asked.

She didn't reply.

"I'll take that as a no. Which is very unfortunate because he was supposed to vet *you* before you actually started working for us, so allow me to fill in the blanks. Sampson is a meticulous organizer. He's also an insane bastard, but he always has his shit together, which includes having a plan B. And C, D, E, and F."

"Your point, Mr. Murder?" she growled.

He narrowed his cold eyes. "Speak to me like that again, and I'll rip out your tongue and mail it to your parents."

"Good luck with that. I don't have any parents, and my tongue only gets me in trouble. Especially with men like you." She paused, noting the room for interpretation. "I meant that in the talking context."

"Do you have a death wish?" He folded his thick arms across his chest.

"Yes, but it's not intentional. I'll shut up."

"Good choice. And now I'll give you the opportunity to make another one; Sampson didn't bring you in by accident. He knew something was going to happen, which means you were given that job for a reason."

She arched two brows, waiting for him to deliver the punch line to his outrageous, senseless statement.

"He didn't hire you to answer the phone, Jane. He needed an office manager, someone to coordinate for the *operators*."

"That makes zero sense. Zero." She held up her hand and made an O with her fingers. "He knew nothing about me or my skill set, so why do you assume he wanted to recruit me?" Sampson didn't even know who she really was. All he got from her was a name, a Google Voice phone number, and an email.

"I never said anything about recruiting you. I *said* he had his reasons for hiring you."

"So you're saying there was a pool of applicants, and he picked me because…?"

"You'll have to ask him that. If he resurfaces."

"Sorry, but I don't plan on hanging around long enough to see how that plays out."

"All right. But consider this: one of the deadliest, most violent drug cartels in Mexico now knows who you are. They have your picture. They know you work for Sampson. At this very moment, they're probably trying to find out where your family lives."

She didn't have any family. Still… "What the hell? I just answered the phone."

"Was that all you did, Miss I'm Having a Heart Attack?"

She threw her head back and groaned. *Why? Why did I have to answer that last call?* She should have just walked away and gotten on the bus to Yuma. *But no… I had to try to be brave. Idiot!*

"Fine." She met his hard gaze, craning back her neck. "They have my picture. So does Walmart, the gas station, and every store I've ever been in. Doesn't mean they can find me." She knew how to disappear.

On the other hand, maybe she was being a little too cocky. She'd only been off the radar for a month. Ed would use his position at the FBI to try to find her. Eventually he'd succeed.

Not if I take Ed down first.

But for that, she needed money, a steady job, and a safe home. A refuge. She needed to be the sort of woman people would look at and say, "She's a good, hardworking person with nothing to gain from lying." She needed to be credible if she was to stop Ed the right way.

More importantly, she needed to stop his

entire operation, each and every link of the chain helping to take those women from the poorest places in the world and lock them up in that building. The videos and tape recordings of Ed's poker night conversations wouldn't be enough. He and his friends had the power to make it all go away—the accusations, the human evidence, the noise. Anyone who doubted that simply had to look at a certain powerful Hollywood producer who got away with some pretty horrible shit for decades. And *those* women—his victims—they weren't nobodies. They had voices, money, and fame. Still, none of that alone had been enough to take him down. It wasn't until the public outcry became so loud that the facts couldn't be ignored and buried any longer.

Emily had learned from that case. It helped her look at every possible angle—what she was willing to sacrifice, how far she was willing to go, what was needed. Ed's powerful friends could shut people up and make the women disappear. If she really wanted to stop him and his men, she needed the world to see the videos she'd made. They had to believe her story. She needed public outrage.

Step one, though, Emily had to get the women, "the living evidence," out of that building safely and bring them somewhere with warm beds and food. Somewhere they couldn't easily be found while the story broke. Yes, time was of the essence—Emily knew that—but if she did this incorrectly, the most important evidence would all be dead, Ed and his associates would walk, and their clients would walk. The world would look the other way, and eventually, the sick and vile business would ramp up again.

Emily looked up at this hit man who, despite his frosty exterior, no longer frightened her. His demeanor was stone cold, his words were uncaring, but there was a vein of honor coursing through that iceberg he called a heart. In short, she'd met worse. She'd married worse.

"Look, Jane, I'm not going to tell you—"

"Emily. I go by Emily."

He paused for a moment, perhaps suspicious of her motives for revealing her cover name. "Well, *Emily,* I'm not going to—"

"And your name is?" she asked.

He gave her a look—shrugged dark brows, his eyes twitching with curiosity.

"Well," she elaborated, "I need to call you something, and Mr. Cold Eyes is getting old."

He hesitated. "Charge. They call me Charge."

"As in, *Charge* it to my room? Charge the castl—"

"As in, I'm in charge. Pleasantries are over now. It's time to make a decision," he demanded.

"No, I'm not staying. The cartel is the least of my concerns right now."

"Then you must be in some pretty deep shit."

"Minus the pretty."

"Ever cross your mind that having forty guns at your disposal might come in handy?" he asked.

"I don't like guns, which reminds me..." She pulled the revolver from the back of her jeans and handed it to him. "Careful. It's loaded. And it has a little ass sweat on the barrel."

He remained with his arms crossed. "I wasn't referring to the physical weapons, Emily."

It took her a moment to grasp his intent. "Oh. You mean," she lowered her voice, *"hired guns."*

He shrugged noncommittally.

"The answer is still no. And even if it wasn't, what the hell could I possibly bring to the table?" She sensed this was the type of business that required more than just understanding how to answer a phone. She didn't know how to vet clients or do anything remotely related to "pest control." Nor did she want to.

"Like I said, Sampson always has a plan. I'm sure he's just lying low until whatever bullshit he's gotten into blows over. Until then, we need someone to help."

"You can't be serious." She resisted laughing. The entire thing was ridiculous.

"We're in the midst of a turf war with the cartel, and the team's plates are full with back-to-back jobs on top of that. We don't have many other options."

"What about vetting jobs?" she asked.

"I'll do it. You just deal with the clients, pass messages to the team, coordinate when we need assistance, make sure our gear is ready and stocked up."

Once again, her gut was telling her to cut bait. The last thing she needed was to get stuck in the middle of something shadier than she was running from. "I'm sorry, I want to help. I do. But I—"

"You'll get Sampson's cut of the money. That's the rule; we all get our piece according to the work we do."

Whoa. She'd seen the files. Sometimes Sampson made a few thousand. Most of the time, he made a lot more. "Why not just run everything yourself, or get one of the other operators?"

"Because my talents are better put to use trying to take care of this cartel problem while we still can. Otherwise, that war raging a half a mile away, on that side of the border, will come here— for good."

Something was missing from his explanation, which she assumed was meant to appeal to her compassionate female heart; however, she already knew that these hit men weren't all about defending the community, like Good Samaritans doing charity work. They were hired guns. She'd seen the files with the dollar amounts paid in exchange for killing a wide variety of dangerous sleazeballs. Sure, they had "rules," but at the end of the day, they were in it for the cash, and this thing with the cartel was only a small piece of their business. Maybe it was even in defense of their business—they didn't want the cartel in their sandbox. Did any of that matter to her? Not really.

"Emily," he said in that deep, gruff, authoritative voice, "I understand this is a big moment for you. In or out decides two very different paths. But if you say no, I can't protect you. You know too much and there are some in our group who wouldn't feel comfortable allowing you to simply leave. Not at a time like this. They might even think you're the person who told the cartel where to find us."

And full circle: There is no out. They'd hunt her down and kill her. Sure, she could run, but this situation wasn't like with Ed, where she intended to eventually expose herself and take him down. If these guys wanted her head, she would never be able to come out of hiding. Never.

Fuck, fuck, fuck! "Fine. I'll do it. But only until this turf tiff is over and you find another person to answer the phones." Between now and then, she'd have to figure a way out. Maybe it was as simple as convincing them she wasn't a rat. Maybe it would be a question of finding some sort of leverage against them. She didn't know. Bottom line, she needed to outsmart them all if she was going to walk away.

"I'll see what can be done," he said, "but I can't make any promises regarding the terms of your employment."

"Yeah, well, I have my own war to fight, and I'm not about to give up just to be your receptionist."

"Office manager," he corrected. "The role is officially office manager."

"Oh, goodie. A fancy title. That changes everything," she rumbled. "So what's next?"

"The operators still have jobs to do—good-paying, *important* jobs—which means the show must go on, no matter what. Find us a new place. Near a main street with alternate routes, no other buildings within a hundred feet, somewhere people won't get suspicious. You have forty-eight hours." He turned and started walking away. "And if I were you, I wouldn't go anywhere near that office. And don't forget your duffel bag."

"Wait. What?" She glanced down at the bag on the ground. It was hers. She just hadn't realized it since it was so dark.

He got it for me? That was thoughtful, but why couldn't she just go back herself and get—

An explosion ripped through the air, rattling the dumpster's lid and making her eardrums howl.

She jumped. "Jesus!" The sound came from the direction of the office. When she turned her head toward Charge, he was gone.

She walked toward the street at the end of the alley and saw flames bursting through the roof of the strip mall. Had the cartel done this?

Suddenly, she heard sirens off in the distance. Cars were stopping and people were video recording the fire on their phones.

Well, I guess now I understand why Charge said to find a new place with some distance between other buildings. Did this happen often?

As she stood there watching the fire grow, she realized that her new life had just become as shady as the life she'd left. Except this time, she wasn't standing on the sidelines. She was the goddamned manager.

CHAPTER EIGHT

Later that evening, Emily returned to her crappy apartment with her duffel bag and more questions than answers, some of which she had to get if she ever hoped to find a way out of this.

In the meantime, she had a few other pressing doubts. Was it really safe to keep coming back here? If the cartel had her photo, should she be running around looking for a new office? Why did these hit men even want an office? *Oh, wait. I guess they need a place to store all of their guns.* Okay, if that was the case, why not store them somewhere else? Somewhere a little better hidden that wouldn't end up burned to the ground if the cartel located their little HQ. If the men needed a place for money to be exchanged, and she assumed it was a cash-only kind of business, then wouldn't it be easier to meet at different spots every time? Say, like, the bathroom at Target or a

Starbucks?

Wait. Hold on. Lots of cameras in those locations. Never mind.

What annoyed her most about these questions was the fact that she had them at all. If these men expected her to coordinate, shouldn't Charge sit down with her and share a few details?

How to get a hold of him would be a great place to start.

She filled her saucepan with tap water from the kitchen sink and put it on the electric stove to boil. Ramen. Again. *I hate eating like a broke college student.* But she'd bet even they had places nicer than this. The old stove and peeling paint on the ceiling were pretty special, but nothing outdid the wobbly toilet, falling medicine cabinet, and shower stall that leaked all over the bathroom floor. Going in there was like playing Mario Bros. *Next level, please.*

And that's another thing. Charge said she'd be getting paid. When? He also wanted her to handle the money. How was she supposed to pay the men? Did she need to buy a safe? Keep records? Something about being the keeper of their cash did not sit well. Charge had made it abundantly clear that he did not appreciate anyone messing with his money. He had threatened to shoot her if his payment was late.

She dumped the brick of dry noodles into the water. *Okay, I'll start a list of questions for the next time I see Charge.* In the meantime, she'd find out where the public library was.

Emily spent the next morning dying her red roots brown and then combing through commercial property listings on the computer at the library. El Paso actually had a wide selection of fairly nondescript, older buildings that had probably housed dozens of different types of businesses over time. The top contenders were a funky brown brick building that had once been a Quick-E Mart. The second was a pink and orange commercial space that looked like it might have been a small real estate office. Or possibly a crack house. Could go either way. Number three was an old warehouse with three loading bays, an office space, and a giant produce refrigerator. She'd only seen the photos on the internet, but the warehouse probably smelled like old cheese. Just had that look about it.

On the bright side, all three properties seemed to be in areas where people wouldn't ask too many questions—along a main road, plenty of traffic, no residential properties nearby where people might be keeping a lookout for suspicious activity.

She sighed, staring at the computer screen. Honestly, these places were all dumps. *I bet I can do better.* She continued her search until she found something more to her liking, a place that wouldn't make her skin crawl and had an actual bathroom. *Gentlemen, your business is getting a makeover.*

She packed up her stuff—notepad with addresses, pen, water—and called for an Uber. Her bank account was getting frighteningly low, but she needed to check out all of the locations, take some pictures, and make notes.

By the time she got to the warehouse—location number three—she suspected someone was following her. A black sedan with tinted windows kept popping up every time she hopped into another Uber.

Maybe I should've brought that gun. It was still in her duffel bag back at her apartment since Charge had refused to take it. But what was the point of carrying a weapon? She simply wasn't a violent person. Yeah, yeah. She could probably manage to point it at someone if it meant saving her own life, but actually puncturing a hole in another person's body? *Eeesh. No.* It was too gruesome to think about. *One more reason these guys shouldn't want me as their "manager."*

As for this black sedan, she had learned a few tricks about how to lose people—a necessity when she ran from Ed, who always had eyes posted at their house.

"Hey, change of plans for my destination,"

she told the guy driving and proceeded to update the drop-off on her phone.

Shortly after, she arrived at the Sunland Park Mall, a busy place filled with shoppers from both sides of the border, from what she could tell from all of the Chihuahua license plates.

I never met a man who could keep up with a woman at a busy shopping mall.

She hopped out, entered the bustling mall, and crossed straight through the food court. Her mouth watered at the delicious scent of French fries. She'd never been so hungry. She wove between shoppers—mostly groups of young women and families with small children and strollers—and went out the door on the other side.

Whoever was following, it would take them a while to realize they'd lost her. By then, she'd be several blocks away, picking up another ride over at the Whataburger. *And some fries. I'm starving.*

She hustled down the sidewalk of the busy street. It was midday, June, and muggier than hell. Her white T-shirt stuck to her body like a wet rag, and a constant trickle of sweat channeled down her back into her jeans. Thankfully, there was no gun there.

She cut through the parking lot of the Barnes and Noble, making sure that car wasn't following. *There's the burger place.* She stepped onto the driveway between the bookstore and the restaurant.

The black sedan came out of nowhere and cut her off, screeching to a halt two feet in front of her.

Her breath hitched. Her stomach dropped into her tennis shoes.

The window on the passenger side lowered, and she fully expected to see a gun pointed at her.

"Nice try losing me. Next time, wait two minutes and come out the same place you entered. Most people expect you to try to cross the mall and leave from the other side."

Emily blinked and ducked down to see Charge's large frame sitting behind the wheel. He wore black cargos and an army-green T-shirt that hugged his muscular chest. His dark hair was covered up with a black baseball cap, making his light gray eyes look even more intense.

"*You* were following me?" she seethed.

"Get in." He jerked his head.

"You're a real asshole, you know that?" She opened the door and slid inside. "You scared the hell out of me."

"Good. Maybe next time you'll be more careful and notice sooner when someone's following you…starting last night, all the way to your home."

I knew I should have switched rides somewhere. But she had been exhausted and desperate to get home.

Emily shook her head at herself and looked out the window, away from him. She didn't like this game he was playing. "What do you want anyway? I still have another twenty-four hours to find us a new home-horrible-home, and I haven't even checked out my top pick yet."

"I have another task for you—an errand I need you to run tonight."

"Sounds terrible. What is it?" she asked.

"Let's see this property first."

"Fine. Suit yourself. Take a right, five blocks down, and then get on the highway heading east."

He glanced at her and raised a brow. That direction was toward some newer developments.

"Hold your judgment until you see the building. Okay? If you don't like it, there are those three other shitholes you followed me to. I take it you want to lease the place, right?" No sense in buying if someone is going to burn the place down and make you move again in a few months.

"A lease is adequate."

"Great. So, any word on our friends? Any new attempts on your life?" she wondered.

"No, but the day is young."

"I have to ask, does it bother you?" In this moment, he seemed so calm and collected. Maybe, a small piece of her was jealous. Knowing that Ed might pop up at any moment and chop her to tiny pieces was like being on a roller-coaster ride made of perpetual stress. There were moments when the anxiety faded to the background of her mind, but it was always there.

"Does what bother me?" he asked.

"People trying to kill you."

"Ah." He nodded, his sharp eyes on the busy street, including frequent mirror checks. "I much prefer to stay on my side of the bullets; but no, it doesn't bother me. The risk comes with the territory."

"Does *that* bother you? The…" She searched for the right words. "Your territory and ridding it of rats?"

"Haven't lost any sleep over it yet, but that's why vetting is critical. It helps if you know what side you're on."

Interesting. "Why did you kill Rick, then?" Not that Rick was a nice man.

Charge's jaw tightened and his lips flattened. She hadn't really noticed before, but Charge was actually a handsome man—cleft chin, strong jaw for taking punches, nice lips. The short black beard was a little too rugged for her taste, and his hair needed a trim, but yeah, she bet he cleaned up nicely. She'd also bet that huge chip on his shoulder and the whole murder-career thing was a buzzkill for his dating life. The ominous vibe was a definite turnoff for her.

"You ask too many questions," he grumbled.

"Ah yes. I forgot about the rules. I will work harder to turn everything I say into a statement, sort of like the opposite of *Jeopardy*."

He didn't laugh at her little joke. Too bad. He needed to understand that if she was going to do this job, she would need at least *some* information. "Okay. No questions. Here's the first statement. It's a fill-in-the-blank. My name is Charge. I killed Rick because..."

Charge growled. "You're pushing your luck, Emily."

"If I'm bothering you, feel free to fire me," she threw back.

He shook his head impatiently. "If you're so fond of questions, I have one for you: What's your obsession with poking the bear all about? Do you *want* to die?"

"That was two questions, but let's just say I'm a woman who's lost her patience with bullies. And bears. I'd honestly rather have you put a bullet in my head than be talked down to, pushed around, or threatened. So no, I would like to live, thank you very much. In fact, it's pretty important that I do, but I've also learned that when you run with vicious animals, you'd better not be the weak little rabbit with the broken paw. They'll eat you."

He chuckled and veered right to hit the on-ramp east. "I knew you'd be perfect," he said to himself.

"Sorry?"

"Never mind. Just watch your manners around the operators tonight. Some of them have short fuses."

"Whoa. Wait. Am I going to have to meet them?"

He shrugged. "Yeah. How else are you gonna know who's who?"

Her stomach churned. "Meeting thirty-nine killing machines does not sound like the sort of mixer I want to attend."

"Don't look so terrified. And you won't meet everyone. Most work in pairs, so only one member of each team will be your contact."

Oh, well, that makes a huuuge difference. "Sorry. I'm busy tonight. Plus, I don't have anything to wear," she said flippantly. "Doing laundry has been a little tough to squeeze in between having a gun pointed at me, getting handcuffed in some guy's car, and trying to save the world's saltiest assassin from dying."

He kept his eyes on the road and shook his head as if to say he wasn't quite sure what to do with her. "I'm sure you can figure something out."

"So, are you one of the men who works solo?" she asked.

"Yes."

She nodded. "How did you get into this line of business?"

"*Stop* asking questions," he growled. "It's considered rude in our line of work."

"Oops. Sorry. True or false: You got into this

line of business after serving in the armed forces, and the CIA recruited you to take care of the type of people who are a threat to society but can't be dealt with through legal means."

"Jesus, woman. You're lucky it's just me in this car."

From his tight grip on the steering wheel, she guessed she'd hit a nerve, one that ran too close to the truth perhaps. "Never mind. I don't actually want to know. If I find out you're some war hero, I might start thinking you're a good guy and forget that I'm here under duress." She paused, noting the exit number. "Take this turnoff and then go left at the light. The property is a few blocks down."

They remained silent for the next few minutes. Probably for the best. She wasn't trying to pick a fight with him, but this whole situation had ground her down to the last nerve.

"Right here. Pull over." She pointed to the Spanish-style stucco building with a red tile roof and arched windows.

He pulled into the small six-car parking lot right in front. "It's a bookstore." His tone was all disapproval.

"Correction. It *was* a bookstore—a really nice one that had a coffee shop inside, so it comes with a small kitchen, an abandoned Illy espresso machine, and a very nice bathroom."

"No. This won't do."

"Why not?" It met every item on his checklist.

"The rent in this area is too high. People would become suspicious if there wasn't an actual business with regular customers operating from here."

"Ah. But I thought about it already. The cartel knows you guys try to keep a low profile. And now you say they know what I look like. Maybe they even know what you look like, since they cased that house yesterday."

"I always cover my face."

"Awesome. So it's just me, then. Anyway, they'll be looking for *me* in every grubby hole-in-the-wall. That is, if they don't assume I've left town. Anyway, this is the last place they'd look for our office. It's a nice clean store in a nice part of town. As for the business, it can be appointment only—so no unexpected customers wander in. We can choose a cover business that sounds upscale but doesn't require health department visits or special licenses. Maybe a private art gallery or something similar? We could declare a certain portion of sales and look completely legit." Hide right under everyone's noses. The Sampson way.

He tilted his head to the side. "Actually, that isn't such a bad idea."

"I'm glad you think so, because this place was also a small credit union about ten years ago. There's a vault in the back where we could store valuables. Were you able to recover anything from

Sampson's electrified safe room?"

"What safe room?"

"The one on the other side of the file room, right next to all the guns and ammo. You mean, you never went back there?"

"No. I never asked to." He frowned. "What sort of files were there?"

"Every job you guys did, including the notes and amounts paid."

"He left that kind of information lying around?" He sounded pissed.

"No, it was locked behind a wall."

He shook his head, but she wasn't sure of the context. Was he irritated because the files existed, or because he hadn't known? "Most of it should have burned up with that bomb, but I'll have to go back tonight and make sure."

That was brave, because the fire department had probably started sorting through the rubble and discovered a bunch of scorched guns.

"Are you going to try to find out what was in the secret room?" she asked.

He shook his head. "I have a pretty good idea."

"What?"

"He had money set aside for our operations—equipment, travel expenses, things we need to do our jobs. Also, money to pay us."

She had been right. Sampson's safe had been back there.

"The bomb probably burned it all up," he added.

"And?" She waited for the bad news.

"And we're going to have to find another way to get new guns."

She stared. "You're talking about real guns this time, right?"

"Yes."

"Oh."

"You'll have to talk to the team tonight and ask them to cough up some cash," he said. "That should tide us over until you can generate more money and get things back up and running."

What the hell was the matter with this guy? First they had her answering phones. Two calls. That was all she got. And the calls were both from the same guy: him. Next they'd blackmailed her into being their "office manager." Now she had to do fundraising for guns and generate cash?

"This is ridiculous," she said. "I can't just wave a magic wand and make money appear. If I could, I sure as hell wouldn't be living where I do, starving to death."

"You'll have to double the prices on all new jobs. It'll slow down business a little, but as is, we have more work than we can handle, which is why our operators are loyal. It's steady work that pays well."

"Okay. So how will the jobs come in?" Was there a Craigslist for criminals? she wondered.

"I will tell you what you need to know, when you need to know it. In the meantime, you focus on getting the things done that I've asked for." He got out of the car and walked toward the building, looking over the outside with great care, even going so far as to knock on the stucco.

She sat there mulling for a long moment. *I'm beginning to feel like this guy is just messing with me.* Honestly, now that she was thinking about it, what did she really know about him? Nothing. He said he worked for Sampson, but how could she know for certain? Maybe he'd killed Sampson. Maybe he wanted to take over the business. *He sure as hell acts like it.* It was a little strange, actually, the way he stepped in and started calling the shots. *Or…maybe he's not a hit man at all.* Shocking how that bothered her, but it did. *Maybe his cover is hit man, and he's really a rival cartel member doing some scouting on Sampson's operation?* Maybe an undercover CIA agent? Or a cop? Or…

He could be anyone.

Emily quickly ran through the facts and stacked them up against her assumptions. Day one, he called claiming he'd done some job. Day two, he showed up and demanded money. Next time she saw him, he killed Rick—

Wait. She didn't actually know for certain, now did she? She'd only heard noises outside after Charge left. Later that same day, Charge returned, and she gave him more money. That evening, he called claiming he was cornered at a target's house. *He* said it was a setup. *He* said cartel men had cornered him. When she arrived, she saw two men sitting in a car in front of a house. But was she absolutely sure whose house that was or that those men belonged to a cartel? No. They could have been two regular guys having a private chat, not wanting to mess with the crazy lady screaming into her phone.

She never actually saw Charge leave that house either. Maybe he was never there at all. Then he caught her in the alley and instructed her to find a new property, but he told her to do so *before* suite forty-five blew up. How did he know that would happen?

In short, all along, he'd been telling her things, and she'd just…believed him. Like a sad little sheep grazing on his words.

She suddenly felt the ice-cold slap of reality across her face. It was time to plug in that brain of hers. In her defense, she'd been blindsided by all the crap going down in suite forty-five, and her head hadn't been in the game. Not this game, anyway. That other game consisted of villains of another breed on the east coast. And, frankly, that was the game she couldn't lose sight of. She had to save those women and shut down that business. Human trafficking was just about the worst thing anyone could do to another human being.

The last straw had been when she'd heard Ray, one of Ed's associates, pushing him to expand their business. Little girls. "There's demand, man. And we don't have to go full-on pedi. Let's just lower the bar a little, yanno? There's big bucks in thirteen-year-olds."

Emily had been freshening up the cheese dip bowl in the kitchen while they played poker in the other room and discussed systematic child abuse for money. She'd had to run into the bathroom and throw up. The next morning, her vague pipe dream of escaping Ed and stopping these animals felt so real, she could taste it. The lame excuses and fear that had been holding her back suddenly dissipated. She already had a plan. She had evidence—tapes and videos she'd made of their poker games. And now she had something to eclipse her fear.

Her goal was still there now, weighing heavily on her mind, but she'd neglected to see what was going on right in front of her. *Something's not right. I mean something besides the other fifteen things that are wrong with working for assassins—if that's truly what's happening.*

The problem now was that she couldn't formulate a plan if she had no idea what she was up against. CIA. Cartel. Hit men. Gang. Crazy person. Those were all possibilities.

After doing a few laps around the building, Charge returned to the car and slid behind the wheel. "I think this place will work. Send me the lease details to look over tonight."

"Should I yell out my window or smoke signal you?"

He held out his hand. "Phone."

She dug out her burner from her purse. She really didn't want to swap numbers with him, since he probably knew how to use it to track people, but there wasn't much of a choice. She handed it over, and he entered his number.

"This is only for emergencies or when I request something. Got it?" he said. "Otherwise, you wait until I see you in person to talk business."

"What if I'm just missing your warm, fuzzy personality?"

He grumbled something unintelligible under his breath.

"Well, if we're done here," she said, "I'm starving and need to find a place that has a dollar menu."

He raised a brow in question.

"My rent is due in a week, and the small amount of cash I managed to set aside for food has been expended on Uber rides."

He leaned toward her, and her entire body went into a cold panic. She sucked in a breath and froze up, her eyes wide.

"Easy now. I'm just reaching for the glove box." He stretched his muscled arm in front of her and pulled the lever. Inside were a few bundles of cash. He grabbed them and shut the compartment.

She remained perfectly still, feeling like her heart might slam its way through her rib cage and out of her chest.

He gave her a curious look. "Christ, woman, do I even want to know what happened to you?"

He was referring to the fact that she was about to scream or cry, all because he'd gotten near her.

"I prefer not to discuss it," she croaked, trying not to get choked up in front of him. She knew she had PTSD, but she didn't always know what triggered it.

He nodded once. "Well, if you ever want a freebie, you just say the word. Perk of the job."

Had he just offered to kill Ed? *No. I'm sure he was kidding.* In any case, death was too good for her husband.

Charge held out two bundles. "Here."

She glanced at the money, but didn't take it.

"Consider it a loan." He shoved the money closer.

"Loan?" Why was the guy who'd threatened to shoot her for these same bundles of cash now willing to loan money to her?

"Get yourself a safer place," he said. "It needs to be in a secure building with several exits on a busy street. The rest of the money can be used for necessities—like real food—and getting the office set up."

"You mean, like pens and coffee beans, or hotwiring the place to electrocute anyone who tries to break in?"

"Yes." He added, "The office expenses can be paid back out of the business's cut of our profits—ten percent. You're on the hook for the rest out of your cut, and your cut is decided by how much work you have to do for each job. Got it?"

She shook her head no, but replied, "Sure. Whatever."

"Good. I also need you to go to ninety-one Alameda tonight at eight. Go around to the back of the building. There'll be a plain white delivery truck with the keys inside. Drive the truck to the Rusty Screw—it's a bar. Make sure you know how to get there *before* you pick up the truck, and make sure you're not being followed. Pay attention this time."

"What happens when I get to the bar?"

"You come inside and have a beer with us."

Us. She assumed he meant the operators. The thought of throwing back a few suds with a group of assassins made her stomach knot. "And I'm guessing that asking you about the contents of the truck will be met with hostility and a reminder that I'm being rude."

"You're catching on."

"No. You're just predictable," she threw back.

He scowled. "Good luck with the errand." He stared at her expectantly.

"Oh. You want me to leave now?"

"I'm not your chauffeur, and I have business to take care of," he said.

She wasn't even going to touch that one. She nodded and slid out of his car. Charge drove off, and she stood there, reeling with a thousand thoughts. Who was this guy for real? What had she really gotten herself into?

She had no idea, but until she did, she would simply have to go with the flow. Carefully.

Maybe meeting the team tonight would offer some insights.

CHAPTER NINE

Emily wasn't sure what to expect tonight, so she went with the worst possible scenario her brain could conjure: The truck contained bodies, and Charge and his buddies were going to have a team-building event tonight to bury them. Or maybe the truck contained crates of dynamite. *I'll wear my Converse just to be safe.* Always be prepared for a quick escape.

She slid on her jeans and grabbed her last clean T-shirt, the red one. Tomorrow, she would look for a new place and buy some necessities. She still didn't know what to make of Charge loaning her money, but she wasn't in much of a position to argue. Until she knew exactly who he was, she had to pretend she was on board. With luck, he'd make a mistake or tip his hand. That said, the more she drilled into the facts—how there had never been proof behind anything he told her—

she was becoming convinced: Charge was law enforcement trying to infiltrate this illegal operation.

Fact: Sampson hired her, and then he dropped off the radar before her first day.

Fact: None of the other operators, besides Charge, had come around the office.

Fact: Charge said he was unaware of the true contents inside those hidden rooms. (Meaning, he was likely an outsider.)

Fact: When she tried to leave her job, Charge claimed she knew too much and she would be hunted if she didn't stay. (Ridiculous. She knew very little when it came to incriminating information. The files she'd seen on the targets contained mostly public information that anyone could uncover if they just took the time.)

So what if…

Sometime between her conversation with Sampson and that first Monday morning, Sampson and his men suspected their team had been burned and they scattered with the wind? And what if Charge and his team of agents figured out their bust was a bust (someone had tipped Sampson off)? All was lost for Agent Charge.

So then, what's the next best thing when you need something to show for months of surveillance and hundreds of man-hours, your entire operation has gone down the shitter, and you work for the government?

I know what I'd do. She would step into the abandoned gun-for-hire business, pose as a member, and collect intel on the customers. At the very least, there'd be *some* arrests. Now, if Sampson and his team were being funded by the local or state government via unsanctioned operations meant to circumvent the legal system, then the "client" arrests would be even juicier. Agent Charge would catch all sorts of high-profile people in the net. A good day's work for him and his team.

It's all just theories, she told herself, *but the pieces fit.* Including the reason Charge had called her for help last night. He'd probably showed up to the job, intending to gather evidence, but found himself being checked out or hunted by Sampson's men.

I mean, that's what I'd do if my operation was outted. If she were Sampson, trying to figure out if they were really burned (and by whom), she would send a fake client into the office and see what happened. If someone showed up for the job, she would take him or her prisoner to get answers. *Who ratted us out? Who do you work for? Etc.* So maybe Charge showed up to the house, realized that Sampson's men were waiting, and Charge called her for help.

But why call her, of all people? If Charge was a hit man, surely he could have called the other operators himself, right? He didn't need her for that. So why call the office when no one would be there at that time of night? No one would answer.

Because he isn't part of Sampson's team and never was. And he knew she was in the office. *The people on his team, watching suite forty-five, told him.* So when they figured out that Charge had been set up by Sampson, Charge decided to call the office, knowing she would answer.

What possible purpose would that serve? The phone had to be tapped. By Sampson *and* by Charge's team.

So she answered. Sampson would be listening. Charge's team could send him a message: *We know it's a setup.*

In her mind, that would get Sampson to abort his little fishing expedition, serving two possible motives for Charge. One, Charge really had been trapped and they wanted Sampson's men to leave, or they wanted Sampson's men to leave so Charge's team could follow—possibly leading them to Sampson or some of his hit men.

Again, all just a theory, but if she was right, Sampson had gotten the proof he wanted; he and his team had in fact been burned. Maybe they knew how, maybe they didn't, but that proof was all Sampson needed to hit the self-destruct button and burn suite forty-five to the ground—a huge issue for Charge and his team because now they'd be unable to continue with their sting operation against Sampson's clients.

Unless Charge set up a new HQ?

And that led Emily to her next hypothesis: her role.

Charge's team needed someone to interface with clients to make the operation appear like it was still up and running. They needed someone who believed they were actually working for the real Sampson and could plausibly be Sampson's assistant.

Someone with no real footprint. The real Emily Rockford was exactly that. She was from a small religious community in Illinois. She had a birth certificate, a social, and a driver's license. The man who'd sold Emily's identity said that she lived on a farm and didn't even have internet—thus the thousand-dollar premium for a nice, clean identity of a woman who'd likely never notice another person living under her name. Anyone questioning who Emily Rockford was or if Sampson had in fact brought her on board wouldn't find much information to contradict the story. She was a perfect buffer between the clients and Charge—a way to appear like the operation was still in full swing.

As for Rick, he had probably been arrested by Charge, not killed. *Caught in their sting net!*

Bottom line, though, if any of her wild theories were correct, she was in deep, deep shit. An undercover team within the government had already started looking into her. Her information and picture would eventually make it into a database. Ed would find her.

Unless I can trust Charge and tell him the truth? Would he help her with Ed?

All good questions, but how to get the answers? If her assumptions panned out, Charge might see her as a threat to their operation. She *really* did know too much.

If I'm wrong, he'll probably laugh in my face and say I have a wild imagination. Regardless, until she knew more, she needed to play along. A safer apartment, maybe something with an armed security guard, was not a horrible idea. Food was also good. It had been weeks since she'd had an actual meal. The dollar side salad from Wendy's with a can of tuna was as close as she'd gotten.

Tonight, however, she would meet the team, and it would be the perfect opportunity to start poking at her theory. She'd read some of Sampson's files. She knew a lot about the jobs the team had done. That information could be brought up in casual conversation, and if no one had a clue what she was talking about, she'd know they were imposters. Not Sampson's men.

CHAPTER TEN

Emily showed up to the graffiti-covered, three-story building around seven forty-five, ready for anything. Dead bodies, dynamite, and everything in between.

She thanked her driver and hopped out of the red SUV. Once the driver left, she slowly crept around to the back of the building. It was already dark out, but the building had security spotlights every twenty feet or so. *I swear I've seen a murder movie in this exact same place.*

Emily peeked around the corner to see what, if anything, awaited behind the building. A single solitary white delivery truck was parked with its nose pointed in her direction. There were no men, no cars, and no security cameras attached to the building.

Okay. That doesn't mean they aren't hiding. She went around to the opposite side of the building and saw nothing. She swiftly moved toward the truck and opened the driver's side door. The keys were dangling from the ignition.

"Who the fuck are you?" a deep voice called out.

She swiveled her head to see a very large Latino man with a big white hat and an even bigger gun hanging off his belt.

Crap. Where did he come from?

Four more men appeared, coming from a door just between two large loading bays.

And there's my answer.

The men came up behind the first guy, all four wearing jeans, guns, and cowboy hats. She had the sneaking suspicion that they weren't actual cowboys.

"I was told to pick up this truck," she said.

"Where's our money?" asked the first guy, who had a dagger tattooed across his neck, complete with bloody tip and the word *Death* on the handle.

Lovely. "Uhhh…I wasn't told about any money. I was only sent to get the truck. That's it."

"Step down."

"Sorry to bother you with this question, but how much money, exactly, did you want for this truck?"

"Two hundred."

"Oh. Okay." She reached for her purse. "I have a hundred on me, and I'm sure I can easily come up with the rest."

The men laughed.

"What?" she asked.

"Two hundred *thousand*." As he spoke, the door opened again and six more men came out, looking like they were there to rodeo. On her face.

"I think there's been a misunderstanding." She stepped down from the truck, but kept her hand on the door handle. "I'll come back later, after you and my boss have had a chance to discuss things."

"You're not going nowhere, *chica*. Not until we have our money." He rested his hand on his sidearm.

They were going to hold her for ransom? *Oh hell no.*

She jumped back in the truck, locked the door, and cranked the engine. The next thing she knew, she was hauling ass toward the Rusty Nail. It wasn't long before the men were following in two black pickups, all three vehicles weaving precariously through traffic.

Shit. Shit. Shit. Heart pounding and hands shaking, she got out her phone and dialed Charge. It went to voicemail. "It's me. You didn't say anything about having to pay these guys, and now they're chasing me. If you get this, I'm heading straight to the bar. Please be there. I don't know what to do." She ended the call and hit the accelerator. Maybe if she was lucky, she'd get pulled over and the men would drop their pursuit.

On second thought... She wasn't sure what was in the back of the truck. *I don't want to get pulled over with dead bodies! Or dynamite!*

The pickup closest to her came up on her right.

"No you don't!" She veered right, trying to run them onto the sidewalk. The driver hit the brakes and fell back.

I have to lose them. People in the movies always drove fast to get away, but speeding would likely result in an accident or the police pulling her over.

She took her foot off the gas and began slowing down. In the mirror, she could see the pickups directly behind her and the drivers having a shit fit, waving hands and shaking fists. *That's right. Twenty miles per hour in a forty.* A slow-speed chase. *I've got a full tank, boys. How 'bout you?*

The first pickup pulled into the right lane again, trying to pass her, but just as he came up, she made a left, cutting off a car in oncoming traffic. She watched as that pickup tried to follow but had to swerve and continue on.

That's one down. The second pickup was still on her tail, so she slowed down again, took another left and then another, effectively putting her right back where she was on the main road. Then the first truck passed her again going the other way. She watched in her mirror as it made an illegal U-turn. *Dammit.* She'd thought they'd be down one of the side streets, trying to catch up to truck number two.

With both trucks back on her tail again, she slowed down once more and waited for the perfect moment to hit the gas.

One stoplight… Green.

Second stoplight… Green.

Come on, yellow!

Up ahead at a busy intersection, the light turned. *Yes! Yellow!* She waited a moment and then hit the gas and sped through the busy intersection, running the first few seconds of the red light. The cars coming from the other direction began filling the intersection, cutting off the men in the pickups.

Woohoo! Yes! Yes! They'd be running that light as soon as there was a window, but she still had enough time to get to the bar, and that sounded far better than driving in circles all night.

She went back to her phone and called Charge again. No answer.

Okay. Think. She'd be at the bar in about two minutes. She could park around back, run inside, and get Charge. He'd know what to do. Wouldn't he?

He'd better. That sonofabitch! Why did he set her up like this?

She arrived to the dive bar in a run-down strip

mall not so different from where suite forty-five had been, with the exception that this one had actual businesses. She parked the truck in the back alley, hopped out, and jiggled the door with the small "Rusty Nail Deliveries" sign.

Locked? Shit! The bar was sandwiched between a bowling alley and a pizzeria. She'd have to go all the way around.

Maybe not... She ran to the pizza place's back entrance, said a "Please God" prayer, and tugged on the door. It opened.

"Yes!" She darted inside, the delicious smell of peperoni and fresh-baked pizza dough hitting her nose. *Food. Food smells so good.* She sprinted between a row of large booths with red vinyl seats, nearly knocking over some guy with a hot pizza in his hand. "Sorry!" She bolted outside to the front and hooked a right toward the bar, jerking open the heavy wooden door.

Panting, she dashed inside and stopped. The place was dark and smelled like stale cigarettes. Twangy country music played on the jukebox. All of two people sat at the long, glossy wooden bar on opposite ends. The bartender was nowhere to be seen. *What the fuck? Where's Charge?* Where were the operators?

She looked around the room, unable to believe they'd bailed on her like this. *Okay. Okay. Don't panic. The truck is parked in the alley. The men in the pickups have no idea where I went. I'll call a ride and wait over in the bowling alley.* As long as the men didn't spot her, she'd be fine.

She bolted outside—slamming right into a huge mass of muscles, falling flat on her ass.

She looked up at Charge and those gray eyes gleaming with amusement. "Seen a ghost?"

"No." She growled up at him.

He offered his hand to help her up, and she took it, squeezing hard as she got to her feet. *Jerk!* She lifted her knee, going right for his crotch. He twisted his hips, stepped around her, and locked her arm against her back. It was an effortless move, like he'd done it a million times.

"What was that?" His voice was low, gruff, and displeased.

"Let me go!" She squirmed, but he was about eight or nine inches taller and had her arm positioned in that perfect spot where any movement caused pain. The pressure forced her to bend forward.

"Just as soon as you calm down."

"That's a little hard to do when someone just tried to kidnap me and your dick is pushed up against my ass."

A moment passed, and then he released her.

She pivoted, the fury taking hold again. "How dare you!" She swiped a fist at him.

He pushed out his hands and blocked her. Again, effortlessly, like he was fighting a harmless mouse.

"You asshole," she snarled. "Don't ever touch me like that again."

They locked eyes for a moment, but it was mostly him studying her, like somehow her outrage pleased him.

"My apologies," he finally said. "My dick just happens to be attached to the front of my body. Your ass happens to be attached to your backside. I meant nothing by it. Now, would you mind telling me what happened?"

The two black pickups screamed down the street running along the side of the strip mall. One of the drivers must've spotted her because the second pickup hit the brakes and came to a screeching stop.

"They happened." She pointed.

Charge turned his head to see who was skidding rubber. "Who are they?"

"The fucking guys who want two hundred thousand dollars for that truck you had me pick up, and who were going to take me prisoner until they got their money."

"I have no idea who those men are. They must've hijacked the shipment and thought they could get some money for it."

The pickups made U-turns in the middle of the street and started doubling back.

"What do we do?" she asked.

"Where's the truck now?" he asked.

"In the alley behind the bar."

"I need you to take the truck and deliver it to fifty-one West Prize Street."

"What? No. I'm not getting anywhere near the truck," she protested.

He grabbed her firmly by the shoulders. The pickups were now at the far end of the lot, barreling towards them. "I don't have time to chitchat, Emily. There's a woman being held hostage—the wife of one of my men. I need you to deliver this money and the truck." He pulled a thick envelope from his back pocket and shoved it into her chest. "I was going to do it myself, but now I need to deal with these guys."

"But what about one of the other operators? Aren't they supposed to be here? Can't they help?"

"The meeting got called off because this issue popped up. Now go. And be sure to bring a gun. You're going to a rough neighborhood, and I doubt you'll be able to get a ride back."

Gun? And he expected her to walk home at night through a bad neighborhood?

The cowboy-hat crew unloaded from their pickups. She could see they were reaching for guns behind their backs.

"Go!" Charge yelled at her and turned to face them.

Oh God. I can't believe this is happening. "You and I are going to have a long talk if we live through this."

"*I'll* live."

Oh, but *she* wouldn't? *Asshole!*

She turned and ran into the bar, cutting straight through the tables and bursting out of the emergency exit into the alley. She slid back into the truck, still unsure what the hell was inside it or what would happen to Charge. But like every event from the past five days, there was only time enough to react and nothing more.

Maybe it was a good thing. Because if she stopped and thought about one second of all this chaos, she'd probably be in the fetal position, hiding under a bush.

Exactly forty-five minutes later, Emily had stopped by her place, grabbed more cash for incidentals (since her bank account was down to almost zero), and shoved the loaded gun in her purse. She honestly hated even looking at the thing, but if Charge told her she needed it, she needed it. Sure, she could run, ditch the truck, and never look back, but if a woman's life really sat on the line, how could she walk away? No one had ever come for her in her darkest hour. No one had cared if she lived or died or took another punch to the face when Ed was in one of his moods. Knowing she was all that stood between such a fate for another human being was something she couldn't ignore.

Emily pulled in front of fifty-one West Prize Street. It was a large, two-story house with white pillars and an enormous Italian-looking fountain centered in a circular driveway. The wrought-iron fence with spikes around the perimeter detracted from the elegance, in her book, but far better than her super-classy efficiency studio with the domestic abuse channel next door. For the record, the woman neighbor gave it to the man most of the time. Still sick.

As for this neighborhood, well…yeah, it was pretty rough: abandoned burned-out cars with graffiti, weeds growing in the cracked sidewalks, and trash just about everywhere. But none of that unnerved her nearly as much as the immaculate mansion smack in the middle of it all. Whoever lived here either had the community's respect or their fear.

Emily pulled into the driveway, lowered the window, and punched the red intercom button just outside the gate. After a moment, a deep voice crackled over the speaker. "Yeah?"

"I'm here with a delivery."

"From who?"

She had no clue if it was okay to say Charge's name. He hadn't given her instructions. "Names aren't any of my business. All I know is I've got an envelope and a truck."

The gate buzzed open.

Guess that means come on in. She pulled forward and drove the truck all the way around the fountain, leaving the vehicle pointed toward the gate. Could she push this thing through that fence if she had to get out quickly? Who knew? But better to have the option.

She took the keys with her this time and shoved them in her front jeans pocket. The envelope was in her purse along with the gun.

She stepped up the front porch to the huge iron doors and rang the bell. The door popped open.

Standing there was a Caucasian guy in a baggy white T-shirt, torn jeans, and army boots. His thick arms were covered in tattoos.

"Well. Hi there." He looked her over like a piece of meat and then flashed a sinister smile.

Her blood pressure hit the roof. His smile reminded her of Ed's dirty friends—the way they used to look at her.

Panic speared the middle of her stomach. Charge hadn't said anything about the threat being here at the drop-off spot, but he also hadn't told her it was safe. Logic said if these guys were holding a woman hostage, they weren't the nicest people on the planet.

She resisted the urge to reach in her purse and rest her hand on the loaded gun inside. She didn't want to draw attention to the only thing that might keep her safe.

Dammit. I really hope I don't have to shoot

anyone. It was a line she never wanted to cross.

The man stepped aside and allowed her to pass. "You can wait in there, sweetheart. Marco will be down in a minute." The man indicated she should go to the room just right of the grand staircase with a gold metal railing and a huge gold-and-crystal chandelier hanging over it. The floors in the entry were all white marble, and the walls were painted peach. Beveled mirrors and photos of lions hung everywhere. Apparently, Liberace decorated the house. *Flamboyant gangster chic.*

"I'll wait here by the door, thank you," she replied.

His eyes turned hard, and his posture went rigid. Maybe he wasn't used to people saying no.

"Look," she added, trying to look confident and not fidget in her Converse, "I'm here to drop off the envelope and truck. I'm not here to socialize."

Suddenly, she wondered what would become of the woman. How had she not thought to ask Charge about this? *Oh, yeah. We had a mob of gangsters barreling toward us.* It had been a smidgeon distracting, but that was no excuse for the last forty-five minutes while she was en route to her apartment then to here. What was supposed to happen at the end of this deal? Would they hand over the hostage or drop her off at some predetermined location?

"Who the fuck are you?" A tall man with thick wavy black hair, wearing a white button-down shirt and black pants, stood at the top of the ornate staircase. He had tanned skin and stunning light eyes—maybe light green or hazel—he was too far away to tell, but what struck her instantly was the coldness in them. They reminded her of Charge, of someone who'd probably killed a lot of people and, in doing so, had lost all human warmth.

"You must be Marco. I'm the delivery person." She lifted her chin, trying to be brave, but her hands were sweaty and her heart was beating like a war drum. *Oh, God. I think I'm going to throw up.*

"Where's Charge?" Marco asked.

"Tied up, I guess." She was about to produce the envelope, but something stopped her. "He said you're supposed to show me the woman first—make sure she's okay. Then you can have what I've brought."

He stared for a long moment from atop his perch, zero emotion showing through that rough exterior. Her sweaty hand started to twitch. Her fingers tingled with the urge to go for her gun. The air filled with thick, stifling tension. She could hardly breathe.

Marco suddenly threw back his head, letting out a husky laugh. "Okay, honey. You want to see the woman? You can see the woman." He waved his hand. "Come on up."

Oh God no. "Bring her down."

"Look, sweetheart. If you want to see her, then you'll need to come up here, because I'm not cutting her loose from that bed until I have what Charge promised."

Emily's heart revolted in her chest. They'd tied her to the bed. God only knew what they'd done to her. *I changed my mind. Now I really do want to shoot someone.*

She growled at the man and then stomped up the marble stairs, giving him a little bump as she passed.

The man laughed. "You're a feisty one. Where'd Charge find you?"

"The want ads," she said flatly. "Where is she?"

"Second door on the right."

Emily marched to the door, consumed with anger. She turned the handle and pushed open the door. Against the wall, directly across from her, was a woman with dark hair and a gag in her mouth, tied to a bed. She had dried mascara stains down her cheeks. To the woman's side, a man with a beer belly and greasy black hair had his pudgy hand on the woman's breast.

A flash of white-hot rage ignited. The ability to think or rationalize left Emily. All she saw was herself on that bed. The pain. The torment.

Emily looked down at her hand just as the

gun went off. She hadn't even realized she'd gone for it. But she had.

And fuck. I missed. Who knew where the bullet went, but at least it hadn't hit the woman.

Startled, the man stood from the bed and stumbled back.

Knowing that Marco was behind her in the hall, probably drawing his own gun, Emily stepped into the room and pushed her back against the wall just left of the doorway. She immediately turned her body and pointed the gun just as Marco stepped into the room, gun out.

In that moment, everything happened so fast.

He pivoted his body toward her. She shot first.

After that, everything moved in slow motion.

Marco stared at her for what seemed like an eternity. She saw the terror in his light cold eyes. The shock, the pain. He couldn't believe she'd put a hole in his chest. Neither could she. It was horrific, ending another person's life. Didn't matter how justified, it was the sort of thing that would leave a permanent scar on her soul. She didn't need hours, days, or years to process it. She just knew.

"I'm sorry," she whispered.

He pressed his hand over the spot, and she watched the bright red stain seep into the white fabric of his shirt, spreading down like floodwater gushing through a ravine.

Her consciousness kicked in, telling her there was still another threat in the room and another man outside. Maybe several men.

She swiveled on her heel and pointed the gun at the big-belly man, Mr. Fondler. "Untie her," Emily barked.

The man scrambled to the bed and hastily began undoing the knots. With her first hand free, the woman pulled the gag from her mouth and started panting.

"How many are in the house?" Emily growled at Mr. Fondler.

"Just the one. Just the one."

"Bullshit!" Emily shook the gun at him. "Don't fucking lie to me!"

"Okay. Okay. Five. There are five more."

"Who is second-in-command?" she asked.

The large man blinked at her.

"Who!" she urged.

"Um. Um…Bruno."

She figured Bruno couldn't be far. "Bruno! You there in the hallway?"

"Yeah," the deep voice echoed outside.

"Well, I killed your boss apparently, which now puts you in charge. You're welcome, by the way. Now, can I have your word that I'll be allowed to leave here with this nice woman?"

Silence.

"I'll take your friend with me as insurance, of course," she added. "But I promise to only break his hand and not kill him for accosting the hostage. That is, if I have your word?"

"I want what's in the truck and that envelope."

"Fine by me. Do we have a deal?" She raised a brow and looked at the man across the room, who was now sweating profusely. The woman was busy untying her foot.

"Yes. You are free to go," Bruno said.

Emily crinkled her nose at the big-bellied guy. "Come here, dickface." It was a good thing that the guy liked his beer because he would be the perfect shield.

The woman, now free, scrambled from the bed and started attacking the guy. "I'll kill you, motherfucker! I'll rip off your balls."

Emily exhaled. "Excuse me. Excuse me. We need to go, but I promise you can do what you like with his balls once we're safely away."

The woman stopped and looked up at Emily, her eyes filled with emotion and despair.

It broke Emily's heart. "Scout's honor." Emily raised her left hand. "But let me try to get us out of here alive."

The woman backed off.

"Thank you." Emily jerked the gun at her human escape shield. "You first, big man. And keep your hands up." She had no clue what she was doing, but this wasn't the time to get out the pen and paper to brainstorm. They needed to get the hell out of there.

Emily pushed the gun into the small of the man's back, and he stepped into the hallway first. She peeked her head out quickly, noting three men waiting for them. *I don't think they're keeping their word.*

She reached behind her, grabbing the woman's wrist. "Run!"

She pushed the large man into the waiting group and turned toward the stairs with the woman in tow. "Go! Go!" They both stumbled down the grand staircase, getting to the front door as the men chased after them. Emily flung the door open, and both of them stopped.

An even larger group waited outside.

"Oh shit."

CHAPTER ELEVEN

Emily thought she'd gone into this evening prepared for anything, but boy, was she wrong. The large group gathered outside the front door looked mean and deadly, like someone had just scooped them up from some commando, Navy SEAL mission from the middle of a war zone, dressed them in Must Have Tees, and then dropped them right on this doorstep.

I think I'm going to wet myself. But as her bladder threatened to betray her, a few very peculiar things stood out from her elevated vantage point on the front steps.

One, she could see right into the truck she'd driven here, and the back was open and empty. Two, the men weren't all men. There were female faces sprinkled in the crowd, too. One was the woman from the other day who'd come into the suite looking beat up. Today, she had on a dark green baseball cap, but Emily would recognize her anywhere even if the black eye was miraculously absent. Three, while the large group of maybe twenty or thirty people looked tough as hell, none were reaching for weapons.

Charge's black sedan pulled through the open gate.

Right behind it were those two black pickups from earlier.

What the hell is going on? With her hand still gripping the gun, Emily watched as Charge got out of the sedan. The look on his face was so insane, so uncharacteristically happy, that she was absolutely certain she had not made it out of that bedroom back there.

Charge walked over, all heads following him as he stopped a few feet in front of the steps where Emily and the woman stood.

"What the hell is this?" Emily snarled.

Charge opened his mouth just as a loud noise exploded through the air. A gunshot.

Everyone's attention turned in the direction of three beige vans pulling up on the sidewalk just outside the wrought-iron fence. The side doors slid open, revealing men with heavy guns. They jumped out, ran up against the fence, and started shooting through it straight at the group in front of her.

Charge's eyes went wide, and he dashed up the steps where Emily stood. "Get down!" He grabbed her wrist and yanked her so hard, she flew forward, cracking the side of her head on the pavers below. A searing pain rushed through her skull, but she noticed the woman still standing at the top of the steps clutching her stomach, blood pouring between her fingers. The woman dropped.

They shot her? They shot her! Emily winced as the house, people, and voices all around swirled into her own private tornado of chaos and pain.

"Don't move, Emily. Just stay down," said that gruff, familiar voice, lying on the ground next to her.

"Not going anywhere," she groaned.

Charge got up and scurried behind his sedan at the edge of the driveway.

She couldn't see straight, but it didn't take clear vision to know that the men in the beige vans were trying to kill everyone who was now taking cover behind the truck she'd driven here and some of the other vehicles.

I'm going to be sick. One man lay on the pavers in the driveway a few yards away. The empty glazed-over look in his eyes said it all. Dead.

I need to get out of here. She thought of those women back in New Jersey. If she didn't make it, who would help them? Who would make sure Ed and his band of violent corrupt buddies paid for what they'd done? But as important as those things were to her, Emily couldn't stop the bullets from flying. She couldn't stop the night sky from spinning. And there was something supremely terrifying about knowing she was about to lose consciousness in the middle of a violent shoot-out. In just a matter of seconds, whatever happened would be entirely out of her control.

Emily squinted across the courtyard toward Charge's sedan. Those cold gray eyes drilled into her, as if he were trying to tell her something. But what?

Black shadows began closing around her vision just as she spotted another set of eyes: Those of the man she'd shot. Marco. He was ducking behind Charge's car, too.

What…the…

When Emily's brain began sparking back to a conscious state, she had the odd sensation that things hadn't ended so great back at the gangster palace. Maybe it was the cold concrete floor pressed to her face. Maybe it was the throbbing ache in her head. Didn't really matter much, now did it? She knew that she had been taken by someone. The men in the van? The men from the house? Charge? But as much pain as she felt throughout her tired, hungry body, it wasn't herself she worried about.

What had happened to that woman she'd

tried to rescue? Had she really been shot?

Emily's eyes fluttered open, and she sat up, taking in the cavernous, dimly lit warehouse space. It smelled like lumber but was basically empty aside from a stack of pallets over by a door with newspaper on the window.

And my foot is chained to... Her eyes followed the heavy steel links to a post a few feet away. The post was made of steel and set into the concrete floor, running all the way up to the metal roof.

Great. I'm padlocked to that? Her mind scrambled, looking for anything to pick the lock—a discarded nail, a piece of wire, anything. But the floor around her was clean, which meant her only way out would be to negotiate with them.

Big problem. I don't know who they are or what they want. She had no idea what had happened back at that mansion.

Suddenly, the memories began pouring in.

She had shot a man. She had watched him die and fall to the floor. Moments later, he was alive and well at Charge's side. That woman, who Charge claimed had worked for the cartel and set him up, had also been in the crowd. Finally, the men in the two black pickups showed up with Charge and were also by his side after the shooting started.

She had been set up. That was the *only* explanation. The entire thing had been some sort of... *Fuck. I don't know.* Her earlier theory had been that these men were some sort of law enforcement trying to infiltrate a group of hit men who'd disbanded. Now, she didn't know what to think. That entire scene back at the house had been fake up until those beige vans arrived.

At least, I think those were real bullets. But she couldn't know for certain about anything at this point. *This is insane. All of it.*

About fifty feet away, the newspaper-covered door opened, flooding the room with blinding sunlight. She squinted and watched three large figures coming toward her. The shorter one—a bald guy in his twenties, with a huge-ass calligraphy tattoo on his forehead—came up on her and crouched.

She blinked at him. "Who are you?"

He pulled back his fist and punched her in the mouth.

Her head whiplashed, and she felt warm blood trickling from her bottom lip, down her chin.

That was not fake. And neither was her anger. How many times had she been hit and said nothing? How many times had she just let it happen? How many nights had she blacked out because her body thought it was better if her mind went somewhere else?

Honestly, she could take the pain, but she couldn't take being a victim. Not anymore.

She lifted her leg and kicked him right in the

crotch.

He fell back moaning, cupping himself. "I'm going to kill you," he grunted.

"Yeah? Well, step in line, dick."

The men who stood behind Shorty, one on each side, started to chuckle. They were both in baggy black pants and plaid shirts. The tall skinny one looked about twenty, tops. The third guy had to be about forty with another face tattoo—two lines of words across his cheek, which she couldn't read.

Shorty groaned for another minute and then finally composed himself. He stood up, bent down, and backhanded her, this time nailing her nose.

The burning sensation shot right down her neck and spine. *Crap. That hurts.* She inhaled slowly and took in the pain like she'd done so many times before. But this time, she wouldn't cower. She wouldn't give him what he wanted: her dignity.

She lifted her chin. "In case you're wondering, my husband hit me every other day for three years. And do you know what I learned from him? (A) he's the biggest pussy on the planet because only pussies beat up on people who are smaller than them; and (B) his IQ was about as big as a chicken nugget. Real men use words. Real men know how to get what they want by working hard for it. You're just a small prick in a big body with a raisin brain." She spit the blood from her mouth onto the floor and then smiled.

He raised his fist and started to lean down again. She raised her chin another inch, staring up at him defiantly.

"Hey, man," said the tall, skinny dude to the right, "if you kill her, she's not much use to us."

Shorty dropped his fist and looked over his shoulder. "Yeah. You're right." He pulled a sheathed knife from his back pocket. "I'll just remove something she don't need and mail it to Charge. That should inspire him."

"So you guys don't work for Charge?" she asked.

The men laughed in unison.

"I'll take that as a no." It wasn't a relief exactly. Charge had put her through some pretty horrible things, all of which had led her here. "Okay. So you hate Charge, and you believe cutting off my…?"

"Your ear," said Shorty.

She nodded. "Thank you. You believe that cutting off my ear will get him to do something. Has it crossed your minds that Charge doesn't actually care about me? I mean, the guy has done nothing but lie and pull me into dangerous situation after dangerous situation. What makes you think he'll give two shits about me, my ear, or any other body part?"

Shorty shrugged. "We don't. But hey, it's still

worth a try."

He leaned in with his knife, reaching for her ear.

"Wait." She twisted her head. "Can you at least tell me who Charge is? I'd like to know why I'm losing something I've had since birth for a man I don't even know."

The men went silent.

Poker faces. "You don't know either." She laughed at the utter absurdity of it all. No one knew who Charge was.

"He's been killing our men," Shorty admitted reluctantly. "That's all we need to know."

"Hold on. Are you guys actual cartel members?"

"What kind of stupid bitch asks that?" Shorty said.

"Are you going to answer or just stand there trying to hurt my feelings?" she threw back.

They didn't reply.

"Okay." She chuckled, fully aware that she was losing her mind—the proof being that she didn't feel afraid anymore but probably should. "Stupid bitch here will take that as another yes. Do any of you know a guy named Sampson?"

The three men exchanged glances.

"What?" she asked.

"That's a trick question; no one knows him," said the tall skinny guy. "He's like a fucking ghost. He wants you dead, you're dead."

So no one knew him either, and now things made even less sense. On the bright side, they seemed afraid of Sampson, which felt like an opportunity.

"Well, that makes things extra interesting," she grinned, "because Sampson is the man who hired me."

The men didn't look so tough all of a sudden, shifting their weight and putting hands into pockets.

"You lie," said Shorty.

"No. I started working for him nine days ago. He asked me to help out answering the phones. Oh, and by the way, I personally agree with the whole 'if he wants you dead, you're dead' thing because I read some of his files. He has killed *a lot* of people. People like you."

"One second." Shorty pulled the men aside out of earshot.

She watched their body language closely— hands waving frantically and repeated glances her way. Whatever that was about, it gave her hope. They might be rethinking their choice to hurt her.

They walked back over. "Tell us where Sampson hired you to work," Shorty said.

They wanted proof she wasn't BSing. *Okay.* But she wasn't sure what was what: Who really hired her? On the other hand, she didn't have any other cards to play. "Suite forty-five."

They put back on their poker faces. She had

said something right.

"Where is it?" Shorty asked.

She sensed a timber of anxiety in his voice. "I'll take you there—no problem—but you have to let me go." The irony of having gone full circle wasn't lost on her. Once again, she'd been kidnapped and was using that damned suite to save herself. *Rick two point oh.*

The men looked eager, like bagging Sampson could result in some sort of notch in the old career belt.

"Yeah, sure, baby. We'll let you go," said Shorty.

She cocked her head to one side. "Sorry to disappoint, but I'm not actually stupid, guys. If you want me to take you there, I'll do it. But you have to make me believe I'll be let go. Otherwise, we can stay here and wait for Sampson to find out you took me." It was a gamble playing the Sampson card in such a big way, but like her dad used to say, *"When you're fallin' off a cliff, you grab for the closest branches."*

Shorty stared and scratched his scruffy jaw. He needed a push.

"Think about it," she added. "You're sitting here debating over keeping *me*—a nobody in your telenovela of guns and violence—or finding out the location of Sampson's office. You're trading a mouse for the bull. My meat isn't a very juicy prize." What the hell was she saying? Her tough-guy talk was lame.

"Fine," said Shorty. "It's the middle of the day. The mall is busy. I'll drop you off with Rolo here." He jerked his head toward the tall skinny guy. "You give us the address, and once we know you've told us the truth, we'll tell him to let you go. But if you lie to us or cause a scene, he'll shoot you on the spot. And, in case you're wondering, Rolo shoots kids, women, dogs—he don't care. He'll shoot any witness standing around."

He'll be too busy chasing me through Sears to shoot anyone. She liked her odds. "Deal."

The tall skinny guy, Rolo, removed a key from his pants pocket and unlocked her ankle. She slowly got to her feet, realizing that her head injury wasn't minor. Every muscle in her body burned with pain, her stomach was queasy, and there was a loud ringing in her ears.

"On second thought," she said, "how about a hospital? I don't...I don't feel so good." She stumbled to one side, but Alfalfa, or whateverthe-hell the third guy's name was, caught her.

"How about you shut the fuck up, or we put a bullet in your head?" Shorty offered sweetly.

See, now there is some legit tough-guy talk. "I-I can get it," she swallowed down the bile, "get it together."

"Good."

But just as she said that, the walls started closing in. "I have a concussion." She knew because she'd had them before. Compliments of Ed.

"She's gonna draw too much attention, man," said Rolo. "Look at her—she's a fucking mess."

"We can't keep her here," said guy three. "Not if it'll bring Sampson."

The Sampson card was backfiring. They didn't mind going after the man on their terms, but apparently they objected to him knocking on their door.

Shorty bobbed his head in contemplation. "Clean her up and give her to Junior."

I hope Junior is a doctor?

Shorty left. Rolo, who still had her by the arm, pushed her down and chained her back up. She considered fighting him, but the room just kept getting smaller and the ringing kept getting louder. "Who's Junior?"

Rolo ignored her.

"Who's Junior?" she repeated.

"Don't worry, baby. He'll take good care of you—like he does all his girls."

No. No. No. They were going to sell her?

A few minutes later, guy number three returned. He pulled out a needle filled with a brownish liquid.

"What the hell is that?" Her eyes went wide.

The guy flicked the syringe. "Just a little H to calm you for Junior, baby. Don't worry. You'll love it."

"Heroin? No, I will *not* love it! Don't you fucking dare put that shit in me!" She started kicking and screaming for help. The two men wrestled with her.

"Sit on her, man!" the third guy told Rolo, who did just that.

Rolo pinned her arms over her head and straddled her body, sitting on her stomach, but she still had her legs free. She kneed Rolo in the back.

"Get her legs!" Rolo yelled.

Guy three grabbed her ankles. She couldn't see what he was doing, but his weight crushed her legs as he sat on them.

"Get off me! I'll fucking have you killed for this!" But her words were empty threats. Like all the times before, she knew no one would come for her. No one would care if she suffered. No one would notice if she dropped off the face of the earth.

But for once in her goddamned life, *she* cared. *She* fucking cared. And she would not go down silently. The days of keeping her mouth shut and simply trying to survive were over. She'd rather die than live in fear one more minute. Those women back in Jersey had merely been an excuse, a reason to tread carefully and keep hiding in the shadows. She kept telling herself it was okay because she had a plan, and the plan required her not to stand up and fight, to do whatever it took to stay alive. *"One day soon, when everything's perfect, I'll go public and Ed will be stopped,"* she'd told herself. But really, she had been hiding behind those women. She had been making excuses and justifying her lack of action.

The truth was she'd been too afraid to take her evidence to the authorities. She was afraid of facing Ed in court. She had just wanted to run away and never see him again. Like a coward.

And look where it got me? She wasn't free. Not from Ed, not from the thugs of the world, and not from her past. Nothing would change until she stopped being terrified and learned to stand up for herself. She had to start fighting instead of running.

She felt her tennis shoe and sock come off. The guy pressed her foot into the concrete, stretching the tendons in her ankle.

"Get the hell off me!" She continued screaming and squirming, but the prick between her toes told her she'd lost the battle.

Not the war, though. Never that.

A burning sensation ran up her leg. "You think that's going to stop me from hunting you down? Do you? I promise I'll get free, and I *will* find you." And after she did that, Ed would be next. No more plotting, planning, and hoping justice would be served in a pretty little box with a bow around it.

The men laughed and released her.

"Enjoy the ride, sweetheart." Rolo hovered over her, looking amused.

She felt her brain detaching from her body, the pain evaporating like a wisp of steam on a hot day.

"Fuck you," she growled.

Guy number three shook his head and grinned sadistically. "Junior's gonna love you. He likes 'em feisty. Then he likes to break them."

Her eyes started rolling back, the drug infusing her bloodstream, carrying her off into a dream. *It's not a dream. It's not a dream. Stay awake. Fight.*

A deafening noise exploded in the room.

She blinked hard, trying to focus and see what it was: Bodies flooding the warehouse. Men dressed in black masks. Gunshots. Rolo lying next to her, blood pouring from his mouth.

"Emily," said a deep, scratchy voice, followed by a slap on her cheek. "Emily? Can you hear me?"

"Charge?" She tried to lift her head, but it was too heavy.

"What did they give you?" he asked.

"Heroin," she muttered.

"Great."

Her eyelids started to close. "Too heavy. They're too heavy."

"No. Don't go to sleep." Charge called out to someone to bring him "the kit."

"Charge?" she mumbled.

"Yes, Emily?"

"Are you really a hit man?" she asked.

He chuckled. "Yes, and luckily for you, I'm the best."

"Oh." She smiled and drifted off.

CHAPTER TWELVE

This time when Emily woke, she had a completely different kind of headache. This one felt like a massive hangover. Her mouth was dry, she was sweating but had the chills, and her stomach was a mess of churning cramps.

Where am I? She opened her eyes, noting the soft clean sheets and warm bed cocooning her body. From the appearance of the room, she was in a cabin—wood-paneled walls, red-plaid curtains, and pine trees just outside the large window.

She carefully sat up, feeling a tug on her hand and something taped to the skin. Her eyes followed the clear plastic tube running to a bag of saline hanging off a stand next to the bed. A log crackled in the fireplace across the room. A few feet from the bed sat a mocha-colored leather armchair and a small round table with a coffee cup, a stack of folded newspapers, and a gun.

Gun. Not good.

Was she still a prisoner? She had a vague rec-
ollection of Charge coming for her, but that
didn't mean he wasn't a danger. Luckily, the
knotted-pine bedroom door was open, leading out
into a hallway. There weren't any locks or bars on
the window either. Time to go.

She pulled off the blanket and looked down at
her naked body. Her blood went cold with rage.
Who removed her clothes? What had been done
to her?

Heavy footsteps approached in the hallway.

Crap. She slid from the bed, grabbed the gun,
and got back under the covers, hiding the weapon
under the blanket.

Charge appeared in the doorway, wearing
jeans and a plain black T-shirt. "You're awake."

His familiar face only provided a sliver of
comfort—at least he wasn't some cartel guy
named Junior.

"How are you feeling?" he added.

"That depends on what's happening." She
glanced down at her covered body.

"Ah. That." He leaned against the doorjamb
and folded his thick arms over his broad chest, the
ropes of muscle in his forearms tensing and
bulging. He liked to do that when he wanted her
to know he wasn't playing around, as if showboat-
ing his male strength gave him more authority.

"I had a doctor—a friend of mine—look you over," he said. "*She* wasn't sure what injuries you had, and you weren't in a very chatty mood."

Oh, goodie. I wasn't raped. Funny how that lifted her spirits. Not, *"I got a promotion, I met the man of my dreams, or I won the lottery."* Nope. I *just wasn't raped. It's a great day.* She really needed to raise the bar.

"Where are we?" she asked.

"About three hours north of El Paso. This is my place. You're safe here."

Safe? She coughed instead of laughing. Her throat felt like she'd swallowed rusty nails.

"Let me get you something to drink—some apple juice is what the doctor—"

"No. Thank you. That can wait." She pointed to the leather armchair. "Sit."

He was about to speak, but as his eyes hit the table, he probably realized something was missing. He nodded and sat anyway, leaning his square shoulders back. Maybe he didn't believe she would shoot him.

Cocky. "Let's start with who you really are," she said.

"With your permission, I'd prefer to begin with something more pressing."

"Okay."

"Are you...*all right?*" His tone was serious and riddled with tension.

She stared, wondering why he'd care. What

was the angle? "Why do you ask?"

"Those men who took you. What did they do?"

"You mean the cartel guys who kidnapped me from your staged hostage situation?"

He let out a guttural groan, but she didn't know what it meant. "Yes."

"They hit me. They drugged me. That's all."

He released a slow breath, looking relieved.

What game was he playing with all this concern over her well-being? Whatever the case, she was done with these games. She wanted answers, and no one was leaving the room until she got them.

"They were very interested in sending my ear to you," she added. "Then I mentioned Sampson and they collectively pissed themselves. So, in light of all that, mind telling me what the hell is going on?"

He raked his fingertips over his thick, dark stubble.

"Well?" she pushed.

"I know who you are, Justine Hays."

Justine. Justine Hays. It was a name she hadn't said out loud or even thought to herself since she'd left New Jersey. The strange part was that hearing it now didn't evoke any deep emotions. Justine Hays was just some woman from a past life who no longer existed.

"Who told you?" she asked.

"No one. Not really. The hit on you—or should I say on *Emily Rockford*—was out on the dark web a week before you showed up and answered the job ad."

Her mind quickly shuffled the pieces. "Ed put a hit on me?"

Charge nodded.

That meant it had only taken Ed three weeks to find out her new identity. "How? How did he find out my new name?"

He shrugged. "Clearly he knew who to ask—not that many people run around selling quality fake identities to the public. But the hit wasn't just for you. There were twenty-six names on the list, along with your picture with red hair. My guess is your husband found out who you went to for a new identity. The guy ran or died before they could get the information from him, but they probably found his inventory list or something."

Oh God. "So Ed put a hit on every name, hoping one of them might be me?"

"I believe so. Yes. And the only reason he hasn't caught up with you yet is because you've been very careful not to leave a footprint—and trust me, I checked."

She had her bank account, but that had been set up through another name and social. That fake ID had cost only two hundred bucks, and she only used it to facilitate a few necessary transactions. She knew if anything ever happened and Ed found out her alias, the first thing he'd search for was bank activity under the Emily name. And, of course, running is difficult if you don't have money, so it was something she wanted to protect with an additional layer of caution.

"So you knew who I was. Did Sampson tell you?" she asked.

He rubbed his chin. "Yeah, well, he didn't have to. I'm Sampson."

What the…? She tried to let that sink in, but it didn't go far. "Wait. So *you* hired me?"

He nodded.

"And then you showed up and threatened me and—"

He held out his hand. "Look. When you applied for the job, I really was looking for someone to just answer the phone—I was waiting for a call from some people who don't like having their voices recorded. *And* I needed someone who wouldn't ask questions or give a shit if they saw something unusual. People who apply to the 'paid in cash' jobs typically don't want to be found, and keep their mouths shut. But when I recognized your name, I saw it as an opportunity."

"For what?" she snapped. The entire time he'd known and had been playing with her life. It was inexcusable.

Charge continued, "I thought: Well, here's a gal who's got some pretty bad people after her.

But she's not out there selling drugs or prostitut-
ing. She's trying to earn some money. Honestly.
She's also managed to get this far and not get
caught. So I thought I'd give you a go."

"Go! Go for what, asshole?"

"You're smart. Why do *you* think?"

She inhaled slowly, letting the pieces free-fall:
Rick showing up with money. Charge showing up
and demanding money. The beat-up woman. The
call for backup. The truck. The men chasing her.
The hostage situation. All of it fake.

"You were testing me," she muttered. "They
were all your people."

"Yes. I wanted to see how you handled yourself under stress."

"But it wasn't just that, was it." He had tested
her trustworthiness when Rick and that woman
both came in and left money in the office, and
when Charge said he needed help, she came
running. A loyalty test.

"What was the truck about? Why did you
have me pick it up?" she asked, feeling the rage
build. He had treated her like a rat in a maze.
Why play her like that? What gave him the right?

"The truck was to test your ability to see a job
through even when everything goes sideways. You
did well, by the way. You kept your wits and
delivered, just as I predicted—which was why I
had the team waiting to come out and congratu-
late you."

Rage. Blind rage. "I'm sorry," she snarled, "but did you just say I was driving around, risking my life for *a test*? I could have crashed! I could have killed someone."

"But you didn't," he said smugly. "After everything you've been through, you tried to save that woman. I gave you no instructions other than to deliver the ransom, but you knew what had to be done. You even killed someone to get her out of there." He chuckled. "Marco says you were a natural. You didn't hesitate pulling the trigger on him. Unfortunately, you didn't get to hear his praise directly because the real cartel showed up."

"What about the hostage being shot?"

His eyes floated down to the floor. "That was real."

So it was all just a game to him, a game that ended in people actually dying. "You sonofabitch!" she yelled, feeling the last thread of her sanity being yanked away. She pulled the gun from the blanket and pointed it at him. "How dare you! How dare you fuck with people's lives like that. As if I haven't been through enough!" He'd put her through hell and then, for dessert, thought he'd drag her into some bullshit with the cartel?

"Justine, *those* are real bullets. Please put the gun down," he said calmly, not bothering to get up from his chair.

"No! You had no right!"

"I understand you're upset, but listen to what I have to say before you decide to blow my head off."

She pointed it at his groin.

"Or that," he added.

"You have ten seconds to tell me why I shouldn't put a hole in your dick. Another hole."

"One," he said calmly, "because I know why you ran from Ed. I did my research, and I am very aware of the kind of man he is—the human trafficking, the drugs, the women he's holding hostage.

"Two, that situation back there with the cartel members was very unfortunate, but we all put our lives on the line to get you back, which says something about our team and the type of people we really are.

"Three, it's time for me to move on. I'm tired. I've done what I can to hold back the tide of criminals terrorizing innocent people who just want to work, raise their kids, and live peacefully. And..." His voice faded. He looked away again.

"And?"

"And you're braver, stronger, and more de-termined than I ever was when *my* Sampson put me through the test." He exhaled. "You are the only choice for my replacement."

What? Was he out of his fucking mind? "Re-placement?" She blinked and started laughing hysterically. What could possibly persuade her to want anything to do with this...whatever it was? She laughed until she could hardly breathe and tears ran down her cheeks.

Charge sat patiently, waiting for her to get it out.

When she was done, he cleared his throat. "May I go on?"

"Please do." She chuckled. "I haven't had this much fun since, well, never, really."

He shook his head at her disapprovingly. "I'm sure you're wondering why I would advocate to have you take over, a person with no weapons training or combat experience—but that's not what this role is about. It's about being able to make the right choices in the toughest situations. It's about putting what's right ahead of your own fear and understanding that lives depend on you to do your job, even when you want to run. It's exhausting work, there are no days off, and you question your sanity every day, which is why the mental resilience needed for this role doesn't come from a gun. It comes from a deep belief in the work."

"You mean, being Sampson—a mystical person."

Charge nodded. "Yes. Sampson is a cover. I'm not saying he never existed, but from what I know, the person before me was selected the same way: through a grueling test, which you passed with flying colors."

I almost pissed myself and was kidnapped. How was that flying colors? "Then why give it up? Sounds like you've found your calling."

"I'm proud of the work I've done, but it's time to move on, especially now that at least one of the major cartels knows my face. They're all out looking for me. And, frankly, I think you're a better choice considering the challenges we're facing. You're quick, your heart's in the right spot, and you'll be able to fly under the radar— you don't fit the typical profile of the people in this profession."

Oh God. I can't with this. The entire thing, minus being beaten and shot up with drugs, had been some bizarre job interview.

Her head began throbbing. It was a lot to take in when your brain had swelling and your body was coming down off drugs. "I don't feel so well. I need to be alone."

Charge held out a hand. "We're in no hurry. Take all the time you need to think about it."

"What if I say no? Will your guys hunt me down?" she asked bitterly.

"I only said that to keep you from leaving. But no. If you turn it down, no one will bother you, come after you, or show up on your doorstep as long as you never say a word. But know that if you say yes, Justine, this is not a role to take lightly. It's dangerous. It's life and death every day. The people who work for you are tough and well trained, but without you, they can't operate safely. They need someone who's smart and organized to ensure every job is vetted, everyone is prepared properly, and all of the angles have been covered so they come back alive. The forty-five in 'suite forty-five' isn't an address or a place, it's a reminder of what happens when we're not on our game."

She gave him a questioning look.

"The original team was comprised of forty-five individuals. We've lost five over the years—a tribute to how tightly our operation is run. We lost another two in that ambush, including the woman who posed as the hostage. It was a failure, and it's something I will have to live with. The forty-five is now thirty-eight."

She'd always wondered about that. Why, in a strip mall with only six office spaces, would one of them be numbered forty-five? "If it's so dangerous, why do they do it?"

"Good doesn't always triumph, Justine. They've all experienced some sort of personal loss, and when you've spent a significant part of your adult life being trained to protect and kill, it's a skill they've chosen not to waste. Also, the money is really good. But mainly, they want to *do* good."

Pffft! "I'm sorry, but please don't try to tell me that a group of hit men—"

"And women," he added.

"Fine. Hit people. Don't try to make them

out as superheroes."

He chuckled. "I wouldn't dare. Superheroes wouldn't show up at that warehouse in the middle of nowhere, drag the man who beat you outside, tie him to a tree, cover him in peanut butter, and let a wild pig have at him."

Dear God. "They didn't."

"He was lucky. There were five other guys guarding the place who were relieved of various body parts, which were sent back to the cartel in Juarez."

A shiver coursed through her. It was too gruesome for words. "Why?"

"Because, Justine, when you deal with animals who have no regard for life, you have to speak their language. And trust me, they're not writing poems. They need to be afraid of us or they won't respect our rules. Rule number one being they stay on their side of the border."

"Why don't you clean the other side up, too?"

"I'd love to. But you remove one cartel, and another fifty takes its place. This is the best we can do until people *here* decide to stop buying drugs and funding them. That said, we don't just take jobs dealing with those guys. You've seen the files."

Yes. She had. There were a lot of bad people—murderers, pedophiles, rapists.

He continued, "Those files, by the way, were burned on purpose. The cartel grabbed one of our guys a couple of weeks ago. At first we hoped he'd taken off without telling anyone, but when his cell turned up for sale online, it became clear that wasn't the case. That's how the cartels know who I am now—I made a lot of noise when I was out looking for him, and word got around. It's why I needed to start pushing for a replacement and rush you through the tests. I can't be effective at my job if everyone knows my face, and I'm the one being hunted."

That would make things a little challenging, yes. "Did you find your guy?"

"A few pieces. Yes." There was no emotion in Charge's voice. "We don't think he gave up much information, though, just the location of that house—which caught us by surprise, since we only just took out the real occupants a few weeks ago. We thought it would be safe to stage that final run for you, but I should have torched the place. A message to the cartel to stay out."

"So, if he didn't give anything up, why burn down the office? Not that I'm protesting. That nasty mall was begging to be bombed, but you had a lot of stuff in there."

"I did it as a precaution." He shrugged. "Those were old files anyway. I moved everything to digital years ago. Those guns were pretty old, too. Practically antiques by today's standards. No electronic scopes. No silencer capabilities. Very hard to clean. And I wasn't about to let them loose on the streets or sell them."

Oh. She hadn't noticed the age of the weapons. They simply looked like big ugly guns to her. "And the cash in that other room?"

"The room was empty—I'd already moved everything. But I have to say, I was impressed you figured out it was even there. I also like your suggestion for the new office—*your* office. Very smart."

He was talking like this was a done deal. Not even close.

"So you see," he added, "everything's been dealt with. Or it will be if you take the job."

Job. Being the ringleader. For a group of assassins.

She looked down at her hands. "I get why you do it—dealing with these animals, I mean. But doesn't killing them make you one of them?"

"Justine, if the lions of the world all decided one day that they didn't want to play their roles, then the diseased gazelle would simply infect the entire herd." He leaned over in his armchair, resting his forearms on his thighs. "The lion has its role to play because it must. The gazelle, the zebra, the boar cannot take its place." He leaned back. "You're a lion, Justine. So just embrace it. Cull the herd. Remove the sick. Because no one else will do it for them, and frankly, I'm glad. Who wants to live in a world full of lions?"

She frowned and pressed her hands to her

eyes. She'd always seen the world in such a different way. Law. Order. Courts. Justice. Those were the pillars of a civilized society. But of course no system was perfect, especially when there were people like Ed who were part of it, determined to use their positions to circumvent the law in service of their own greed. So what happened then? What happened when the system failed?

"Can I think about it?" she muttered.

"I believe that's a wise decision. May I have my gun back now? It's the only one I brought."

She gave him a look.

"It's my weekend home. I don't actually like having guns here—they just remind me of work," he explained.

Interesting. She gave it over, grip first.

He took it and shoved it in the back of his jeans. She'd never understand how that was comfortable for anyone. Having a loaded gun pointing down your ass crack was like carrying an arrow up your nose.

"I'll go get you something to drink and a sandwich. You rest." He turned to leave.

"Charge?"

"Yeah?"

"If I say yes, what happens to those women? What happens to Ed and his crew?" Charge said he knew all about them, and she was determined to take Ed down. Nothing could get in the way of that. Nothing.

Charge smiled. "Anything you like." He paused. "Just remember though, you might lead the team, but you don't own them. Their loyalty is predicated on following the rules, one of which is never using them for personal vendettas or gain."

She'd very much like to hear more about the rules, but only if she decided to go forward with this. "I understand."

"Knew you would." He left her alone with the crackling fire and her thoughts.

She finally had the truth, but that didn't mean she knew what to do with it.

CHAPTER THIRTEEN

Sleep was a beautiful thing. Especially when she hadn't had much of it for the past few years. Charge had returned with a simple meal—canned soup and a ham sandwich—and then removed her IV. Honestly, it was the first time in a long time that she could remember anyone caring for her. He even offered her some painkillers, which she refused. "No. I don't want anything else in my body." Not that she worried about becoming an addict after one dose of heroin. If anything, the entire horrific experience would prevent her from ever going down that path.

After a day of rest, food, and lots of sleep, she finally had the energy to get out of bed. Charge came in with scrambled eggs and orange juice.

"Do you have anything clean I can wear?" He'd already loaned her his robe—a huge blue thing that dragged on the floor—for getting up to use the bathroom. "I'd like to take a shower and go for a walk. Looks nice outside."

"Sure. I've got a few things my ex left behind."

Charge had an ex? It was weird thinking of him having a life outside of work, or showing romantic affection. For one split second, she wondered what it would be like to kiss him, but then quickly laughed it off. She would never be able to trust him. Not fully.

"I'll take whatever you've got. Thank you," she said.

He left the room and returned a few minutes later with a pair of pink sweatpants, a pink tank top, and a pink hoodie.

She raised one brow.

"She liked pink," he explained.

"I see that."

"Well, you know where the bathroom is. There's a new toothbrush in the medicine cabinet. Help yourself to my bodywash and shampoo."

"Just as long as it's not Old Spice."

He frowned. "I have to run an errand. Don't go anywhere until I come back."

"Are you scared someone's going to find us?"

"Scared? Never. Cautious, always." He left the room, and she heard an engine outside starting up a few moments later. She ate her breakfast and then took a shower that lasted as long as the hot water. It was incredible. She would never take feeling clean for granted again. Even if he *did* use Old Spice.

She wrapped a towel around her body and then wiped the steam off the mirror.

"Oh God." She covered her face and then slowly lowered her hands. Staring back at her was someone else. Dark circles under her green eyes, a black eye, and bruises on her lip and cheek. Her skin was a sickly shade of white.

How is this me?

A heavy pit formed in her stomach. Then it grew and grew until it no longer fit. She got down on her knees and threw up the contents of her breakfast in the toilet. Hot tears burned her raw cheeks.

After there was nothing left, she got to her unsteady feet and cleaned up, brushing her teeth twice. She didn't dare look in that mirror again.

When Charge returned about an hour later, she was sitting in the living room slash kitchen area. The cabin really only had four rooms—the great room, two bedrooms, and a bathroom. The pine panels on the walls had the typical rustic decorations she'd expect to see in a mountain hideaway—old chipped ceramic pots, antique snowshoes, and a few glassy-eyed buck heads staring off into the abyss.

She wondered why he'd brought her here. Why not a hotel? Why not a rental home? Why to his place?

He wants me to trust him. He was pulling back the curtain just enough for her to see the human side of Charge.

Charge walked in with a bag of groceries in one arm. He immediately spotted her on the sofa in her pink outfit.

"I brought some supplies. You ready for that walk?" he asked.

"No."

He set the groceries on the breakfast bar. "Not feeling up for it after all?"

"I meant, no, I'm not taking the job."

He turned slowly, his face giving nothing away.

"Look, I'm sorry," she said, "but I'm not the right person for this."

He folded those thick arms over his chest. The authority pose. "Why do you think that?"

Because she never wanted to look in the mirror again and not recognize herself. "I've had enough of being beaten to last a lifetime, and I don't want to go to work every day seeing people shot, dying, or bleeding. It's not the sort of thing I want to build my life around." She thought of her father and his saying about the beekeeper. Eventually, they get stung no matter how careful.

Charge rested one hand on his waist and blew

out a breath toward his heavy black boots. "Okay."

"Okay what?"

"Okay. I respect your decision." He walked around the counter and started putting the groceries away in the fridge.

Was he trying to play some sort of mind game? Why would he give up so easily? "You're not going to threaten me or talk me into it?"

"I don't agree with your choice, but I respect it."

"So then what happens to you? Will you stay?" she asked, not at all convinced he was going to let her off the hook so easily.

"I have to. At least until I find someone else."

"Good. Because I'm hoping your offer to deal with Ed still stands." She had no money, and she knew they didn't work for free, but Charge had once offered her a freebie. She just didn't know if he'd been joking. "Actually, to be clear, I want Ed's entire crew taken out, too. Every one of them."

Leaving the fridge door open, Charge faced her, frowned, and then chuckled, like she had some nerve even bringing it up. "Do you have a million dollars? Because that's how much money you'd need to hire us for a job that complex."

"After everything you put me through, including nearly having my ear sliced off by one of your cartel friends and getting injected with heroin—

all because *you* decided to mess with *my life* for a secret job interview—I think you owe me. And what about all that talk about helping people who've been let down by the system and—"

"My guys still gotta eat. They still have bills to pay. Some even have families to think about. And even if they were willing to do it for free, which I guarantee you they're not, there are equipment costs, guns, ammo, rental cars, hotel rooms, and travel expenses. A job like that would take three or four months to set up right—the goal, of course, being to eliminate the targets, leave no trace, and get everyone home safely."

"But didn't you say if I took the role, I could have Ed taken care of? Free?"

"There's a difference with you being the boss and needing to eliminate someone actively hunting you, who also happens to be a very dangerous person, and you just asking for a freebie as a civilian."

It dawned on her that he was dangling a carrot. "You knew, didn't you? You knew exactly how this conversation would play out and that you might be able to entice me to take the job if there was something big in it for me."

He flashed a sly grin and shrugged his broad shoulders. "The thought occurred to me." He returned to putting away the groceries.

She narrowed her eyes at the back of his head. She hated to be played, but she had to admit,

Charge was good at it. Still, "Never trust a hit man."

He closed the fridge door and faced her. "Look, Justine—"

"Emily. Please just keep calling me Emily."

"I wouldn't recommend that. Your cover is blown."

"Justine is just as unsafe to use, and I like it way less." She never wanted to go back to using that name.

"Whatever you want, but do me a favor and at least pick a different last name—something extremely common—Jones, Brown, Smith, Willis. Makes it harder to track you."

"I'll take that into consideration when I go on the run and stop by the false identity store again."

"Don't do that, either. Those guys sell the same identity to a hundred different people. Next time, search for people no one will miss. Then you file for a social security card and start building your own identity." He explained quickly about how she could hire a crooked lawyer to make record corrections with the Social Security Office to reinstate a person's identity after they'd been erroneously declared dead. Apparently, that stuff went through a smaller department that tended to rubberstamp anything that came from a lawyer.

Interesting. "Thanks for the tip."

He dipped his head.

"But I still can't take the position. Not even to

take down Ed."

"What's your plan, then?" he asked.

"I'm not sure, actually." She had the video evidence safely hidden, but her plan to get the women out first and hide them was idiotic. Honestly, she hadn't thought the plan through at all. She saw that now. There was no way one person—her—could pull up and grab them all, then run. Also, as she'd recently discovered, this slow boat to deal with the whole thing had really just been her way of avoiding confrontation altogether. "The problem is if Ed gets wind of anything, they'll take those women, shoot them, and throw them in the ocean."

Charge stared with his trademark Mr. Cold Eyes look, like he couldn't give a shit.

"Really? You really don't care?" she scoffed.

"Never said that. But if I tried to fight every war, right every wrong, I wouldn't accomplish much."

She stared back. She understood, but she didn't agree.

"Look, Emily, if you want our help, you know the price. Otherwise, I'll make lunch. Afterwards, you can tell me where to drop you off."

Her mouth fell open. "Just like that? I don't want your job, so you're just going to dump me at the nearest bus stop?"

"If that's where you want to go, then yes." He pulled out the bread from the cupboard and started making sandwiches.

Meanwhile, she sat stewing. There had to be a solution to all this. She could feel the pieces wanting to fit together. These people could help her get the women out safely and take down Ed and his crew. After that, she'd be free. She would never have to be afraid of her husband getting released from prison. She wouldn't have to look over her shoulder and live on the run.

All I need is money.

A thought hit her like a lightning bolt. "Ed has over a million dollars cash," she blurted out. "I don't know where it's hidden, but if your team caught him, wouldn't we able to persuade him to tell us?" She had to admit the idea of watching him get tortured wasn't entirely unappealing. The peanut-butter-wild-pig thing sounded good. Very *Hannibal.*

Charge looked up from the counter. "That's not how this works. Clients pay up front. Too many things could go wrong."

"But I know the money's there, Charge. I've seen the cash come and go. One of his guys showed up weekly with a big bag. Ed would always take it with him and say he was going to the gym, then work. It can't be far."

Charge shook his head.

"Why is it up to you?" she asked. "Shouldn't your team have a say in this? I mean, it's their risk. Their time. How many people would we need to get the job done, anyway? Four? Five?"

"Ten if we had our normal time to prepare. Which we don't; the team is booked up for the next six months."

"Wow. They're in high demand." She would never admit it, but she was curious who was on the list of upcoming jobs. Who'd slipped through the cracks of justice?

"Yes. They are. There's only a small window next week—the target decided to take himself out, drinking and driving."

"Then give me the slot. Let me ask the team if they want to take the risk."

"You'd need twenty people to get the job done that quickly, and even so, I'm not sure it'll be enough. There's surveillance to set up, which means equipment has to be put in place, and that's not the sort of thing where we can call up and say, 'Hi. We'd like to bug your car, office, and home. Mind if we stop by around two?' Then there's the observation period where we track people's schedules, the sorts of weapons they carry—if any—and decide on the optimal strike situation. Then there's waiting for the optimal situation to present itself, the execution, and the cleanup—removing all signs we were there. It sounds easy, but the work requires meticulous planning, and your job has the added complexity of the women you're trying to extract and relocate."

Did he just say that sounded easy? It sounded fairly complicated compared to her understanding of how hit men worked. Get in. Shoot. Get out. But that was what she'd seen in the movies.

"All right," she said. "I get what you're saying, but you have a shortcut: me. I can tell you who the players are, where they live and work, what their routines are, and when they all meet. That'll cut down on prep time, right?"

The only thing she didn't know was what to do with those women. She'd originally thought—stupidly—to put them up at her place while the situation played out in the media. Then she'd hoped the women would be put under witness protection or something. With this new plan, there'd be none of that. The women would need medical support and therapy. They'd need immigration status and jobs if they wanted to stay. Some would likely just want to go home and see the families they were stolen away from. How did you get someone home who was brought to the US against their will?

"Please. Let me talk to your team. If they say no, then you'll never hear from me again." Either way, she wasn't going to end up friends with these people. If they said yes, she still didn't want to be a permanent fixture of his world. Simply put, she wanted Ed and his men gone. Then she wanted to find a quiet place to start over. She wanted to heal and rest and try to get back everything that had been stolen from her. No more violence. No more criminals. *And more importantly, no more fucking guns.*

Charge groaned with annoyance. "Fine. If you want to pitch, then go ahead, but I reserve the right to pull the plug for any reason I see fit. It's my job to keep them as safe as I can."

"Thank you!" She hopped up, wanting to run over and hug him, but stopped herself. He'd probably stab her with a kitchen knife out of instinct.

"I'll set up the call tonight."

"Thank you, Charge. I mean it."

He shrugged and got on with making lunch.

Meanwhile, it dawned on her that she would have to get on a call tonight with a group of hired guns—people who killed for a living—and try to convince them to do a job on credit.

A cold sweat erupted down her back. *You can do this. You can...*

But what if they said no?

CHAPTER FOURTEEN

Sitting at the breakfast counter, Emily observed Charge setting up his laptop on the butcherblock surface, connecting it to an expensive-looking sat phone. She watched with curiosity as he punched in a bunch of codes on both devices, which brought up a screen with little squares.

"Zoom? Are you joking?" She flashed a look at Charge.

"No. This isn't amateur hour," he grumbled. "Note the silhouettes."

Emily leaned toward the screen, squinting at the blurred-out images. "Oh. I thought you just had bad reception."

Charge looked like he was about to roll those cool gray eyes, but he didn't. "Everyone's here."

They were very punctual. It was eight o'clock on the dot.

He hit a button on the laptop. "Good evening. Sampson here."

Sampson. He called himself Sampson when he addressed the team. Did they know he was Charge *and* the boss?

No. Of course not. The whole Sampson persona was dependent on him being a ghost.

"Like Charlie from *Charlie's Angels*. Can they see us?" she whispered to Charge.

He shot her a look with his hard eyes, telling her to be quiet. "Roll call," he said.

The blurry people in the squares began sounding off:

"Operator four. Kite. Alpha. Two. Butter."

"Operator five. Whiskey. Marmalade. Chipmunk. Five."

She laughed and covered her mouth. What the hell was this? *Sounds like they're reciting very avant-garde haiku.*

But as everyone sounded off, she realized that Charge had a little device in his hand, flashing random images and numbers. He entered each abbreviation—"KA2B" for example—then the device lit up green. It was some sort of verification system with revolving codes.

Some high-tech gear there.

When they got to operator twenty, Charge paused, bowed his head for thirty seconds, and then went on.

A moment of silence for one of the operators they'd lost. She surmised they only did it once because he hadn't paused for operators one, two, or three, and when they got to thirty, they just skipped over it. It was strange to think that a fallen team member was only given thirty seconds of silence, but on the other hand, it was more than she'd expected from hit men—hit people. Whatever. Roll call had nearly ended. Charge hit a button, and he read off his own call sign. Operator forty-five.

The button is to modify his voice! She got it now. Also interesting: Charge was the newest member, not the oldest.

He hit the button again and got to business—as Sampson. He was really good at playing the two different parts, a necessity to keep anyone from knowing he was Sampson.

"All right, team. We've had a few tough days here, but keep your eyes on each other's backs. Things are picking up with our friends south of the border, but it's nothing we haven't dealt with before, and we have some big jobs coming up."

Everyone gave a "huzzah!"

"Also," he added, "I am sorry to inform you that while Emily passed our tests with flying colors, and many of you stepped up—putting your lives on the line to get her back—she has refused the role of operator."

No one said a word, but a flitter of guilt danced in her stomach. No doubt it was the effect Charge was going for. Did he think he could guilt her into changing her mind? Also noteworthy was the little lie. She had refused to be the new Sampson, not an operator. But of course, Charge would never reveal the real Sampson. Also interesting was that it appeared everyone had to pass a similar test to be part of the group. *How oddly egalitarian for a bunch of hired killers.*

He went on, "Thank you to everyone who assisted in her tests, especially Charge for leading this round. I am continuing to actively seek out new operators, so expect more tests in the upcoming months."

Did he just thank himself? She supposed Charge did need to treat himself like any other team member.

Charge continued, "And now onto the other purpose for this meeting. Emily has asked to call in and pitch a job. Hold one moment." He pressed another button on his laptop that brought up the mute sign. He looked at her. "Wait until I tell you to talk. Understand?"

She nodded.

"Good." He pulled out his cell, punched in a very long stream of numbers, and then handed the phone to her. "Talk. You have thirty seconds. Not because I'm a dick but because that's the length of time it takes for a cell tower to pinpoint your location and register it is an actual call versus a dropped signal. Got it?"

"Thanks for the prewarning about the time

limit," she snarled. Had she known, she would have rehearsed.

He ignored her, pressed the call button on his cell, and handed it over. She watched as a new blurry square popped up on the laptop screen. She was dialed in.

Charge gave her a nod.

"Hi, everyone. I know I don't have a lot of time, but before I say anything about this potential job, I want to thank you for coming to help me. I don't know what I would have done if you hadn't. No. Wait. Stupid thing to say. I'm sure I would have died. Likely by my own hand because I'd prefer that over being trafficked. But the point is you came, and now I'm asking you to come again." She winced. "I'm sorry. That sounded really bad, but you showed up, and I'm asking you to show up again. There are twenty women being held in a house near Atlantic City. They were stolen from their parents, brothers, sisters, and children."

Charge yanked the phone from her hand and gave her the cut-throat sign.

I'm not done! She puckered her lips and yanked it back. She hopped up and scurried down the hall. He followed, trying to force the device from her hand as she ran toward the bathroom.

Her voice frantic, she continued, "The women are forced to take drugs and are abused for money so that men like my husband can buy a new pair of golf clubs. I just want them to be stopped! I want them to suffer and pay for the pain they've caused us. He has one million dollars hidden, and it's yours if you he—"

Charge caught up with her, grabbed her wrist with two hands, and gave it a squeeze. The phone dropped, and he caught it. He pressed the end button.

"Why did you do that?" he growled.

"I'm sorry." She hung her head. "I just wanted to convince—"

"I know what you wanted!" he yelled. "But you put us all at risk for it!" He started walking away, visibly pissed.

"I'm sorry," she said, following behind him. "I don't know what I was thinking." Actually, she did know. For that one brief moment, she was thinking about Ed dying. She could see it unfolding in her mind—the look on his face, knowing his pathetic life was over, that he would never raise a hand to her again. He would never tie her up in the closet like an animal and make her piss her pants. And she saw herself holding the gun, smiling, feeling the sweet release of her pain as the bullet flew and shattered his skull. In the blink of an eye, she'd lost herself in the need for revenge.

Frankly, it terrified her. It meant she was not in control of the rage inside her—just one more reason she had to get away from all this.

"Charge, I'm sorry. I didn't mean to do that." She reached out, hoping to get him to listen, but the moment she touched his back, he whipped around and slammed her against the wall.

The rage in his eyes made her heart stop. For a second.

"Don't." He pointed an angry finger in her face. "Don't ever do that again. It's not just you I'm responsible for, it's them, too."

Her insides shaking, she inhaled slowly. "I know," she said quietly. "I'm just really fucked up inside, and I don't know how to fix it." She drew a breath, fighting the tears. "It's why I can't take your job, Charge. I'm not brave like you, strong like you."

"You grabbed a gun, jumped into a fucking cab, and tried to rescue me. You never ran from anything I threw at you." Suddenly his eyes were on her lips, and his voice quieted. "You're the bravest woman I've ever met."

The moment instantly turned to something else. Their bodies were pushed together, pumping with adrenaline, both sets of lungs breathing hard. His solid body against her soft everything triggered something intense and deep inside her core. It was so totally unexpected that her breath hitched.

He suddenly snapped out of it, releasing her with a slur of cuss words, then, "I need to finish the call. Go to your room."

She glared at the back of his thick head of dark hair. "I'm not your child."

"Then stop acting like it!"

He returned to the living room. She went to her room, needing a breather after—well, whatever *that* was. She also knew that pushing him any further would only lower her chances of getting his support for this job. Bottom line though, she'd said her piece. Whatever happened now was out of her hands. They were either in or they weren't.

God, I hope they say yes. If not, she had no idea how she'd ever get those women free *and* stop Ed from obtaining more "inventory," as he called them, some too young to survive the brutality. They'd never stand a chance.

A half hour later, Charge knocked on the bedroom door. She closed her eyes and inhaled slowly. No matter what he said, she needed to be respectful and keep her cool. She owed him that. He had at least given her the opportunity to make her case, and he had been instrumental in saving her life. Of course, it wouldn't have needed saving if he hadn't pulled her into a real-life episode of *Narcos.*

"Come in," she said.

Charge entered, bringing with him a gust of

cold vibes. She could tell he was still reeling from her little stunt. "They said yes."

Her jaw dropped, and her heart soared. "They did?"

"One condition," he added. "If the money's not there, they'll shoot you."

She laughed, but he wasn't laughing with her. "Oh shit. You're serious."

He folded those big arms over his chest. The authority move again. "They're going to put their lives on the line for this, and they need to know you're not jerking them around. If you fully understand that you will be executed if the money's not there, then they'll do the job on credit."

Her mouth twisted to one side. Basically, he was saying that if she was willing to stake her life on that money, then they were, too.

Well, she wasn't lying, and she would bet her life on that money being somewhere near her old house. They *would* find it as long as they were able to make Ed give up the location. But, more importantly, this was happening. They were doing the job!

"Agreed." She folded her arms over her chest, mimicking his pose. "They may shoot me if the money isn't there."

He didn't react or seem to care one little bit about this term of the arrangement. It was strange how he could turn his emotions on and off.

"Good. Then we start preparations tomorrow after they finish a job in the morning." He pulled a pad of paper from the back of his jeans and tossed it on the bed. "Make notes. List the names, physical descriptions, roles in the organization, official jobs, anything else you know about them." He turned to leave.

"Thank you!" she blurted out. "I really mean that."

"Don't thank me. It was the team's decision."

"Yeah, but I bet they don't do anything without a nod from you," she pointed out.

He toggled his head noncommittally.

She smiled. He *had* helped. That little vein of heroism running through his cold heart was larger than he let on.

"Get to work," he grunted, and started to leave again.

"Can I go with them?"

He looked over his shoulder at her. "Absolutely not."

"I want to be there. I want to make sure Ed knows."

"Knows what?" he asked.

"That karma finally showed up for its pound of flesh."

"He'll know. I'll make sure of it," he said, his voice an octave lower.

"You're going?"

This time, Charge didn't bother to look at

her. "Absolutely." There was a sinister growl in his tone, like he was out for blood.

It took her by surprise.

Charge left, and she stood there digesting. Somehow this had become personal to Charge. She didn't know why, and she doubted he'd ever tell her. Maybe he simply didn't like the Eds of the world.

Or maybe it was like he said: the people on the team had all experienced some kind of personal loss that drove them to do what they did.

CHAPTER FIFTEEN

Emily spent the entire night and the next morning, too, making detailed notes about Ed and his men. There were eight primary people besides her husband. One guy handled "new inventory." Two managed the existing girls—keeping them in line and drugged. Another handled "customer service," talking to clients and managing bookings. One handled the housekeeping and maintenance staff—a few people who were probably threatened to work there, but preferred not to. Two more men were in charge of security and collecting payments. Cash only. She wasn't sure, but she thought those guys also handled women who needed to be "fired." That's what she'd heard them call it on poker night. Her guess was they just took them out on Ed's boat, put a weight around their ankles, and dumped them in the ocean.

The building where the girls "worked" and "lived" was located about ten blocks west of the casino strip in Atlantic City and was officially registered as a "members-only poker club," where no one would bat an eyelash at the people coming and going at all hours. Still, the location alone wasn't enough to ensure things ran smoothly. Ed also kept tabs on the Gaming Commission, including possible surprise inspections by officials not on the take.

Ed's brother, Merrill, a cop in Atlantic City, helped out from time to time when clients got out of hand. Those two guys got a bigger chunk of the profits because of their riskier roles. Twenty percent each.

By the time she was done with her notes, Charge had information pertaining to the group's favorite sandwich shop, the cars they drove, and their music preferences. When one spent every Wednesday night for three years listening to these assholes mouth off after too many beers, on top of hanging with their wives at parties, you learned a few things. She'd learned to listen.

Most importantly, she'd learned that the more they drank, the more they blabbed. Sloppy as hell. Which was exactly why she'd started stocking up on top-shelf whisky and vodka and kept the drinks flowing until they'd nearly pass out. She'd even researched what kinds of snacks make a person feel drunker. Basically, no carbs. Nothing spongey to slow the absorption of alcohol. Chicken wings, pigs in a blanket, or prosciutto-wrapped cheese. Not only did the guys think she was pampering them, but Ed usually gave her a break from the beatings.

"Good job, babe. Good job." Then he'd pass out.

God, I so want to be there and just punch him in the balls one time before he dies. Emily finished the last page of notes, forty-five altogether. Not on purpose—that was just the way it landed—but she took it as a good sign.

Exhausted from having zero sleep, she got up from the armchair and plopped down on the bed. Just a quick nap. Then she could go over everything with Charge.

When she opened her eyes some hours later, Emily instantly knew something was off. The light coming through the window was bright—midday—her notes were missing from the small table, and there was one piece of paper in their place.

She scrambled from the bed and grabbed the letter. Her eyes scanned the lines frantically. The pit in her stomach grew larger with each word:

Emily,

I understand that you are no longer accustomed to taking orders from anyone, and while I respect that, I am asking you to do this one thing. Please. As a favor to me. Stay here. Do not go to town. Do not call or talk to anyone. Do not use your phone to surf the web and scan the news. You never know who is monitoring search terms.

If you can't do it for me or even for your-self, then do it for the forty-five. There is no room for error or surprises on this job, and Ed is looking for you, which means the FBI is looking for you.

If you don't hear from me in ten days, take the money, the gun, and the envelope I left in the drawer under the microwave and run. Forget Ed. Forget the women. Move on.

Trust me when I say that living for vengeance means living for your enemies. It taints anything you have left, including the good memories.

Keep this photo safe for me. Take it with you as a reminder of what I said. – C

She reached inside the envelope. There was a small photo of a beautiful blonde girl in her cap and gown. Emily looked closer. The girl couldn't be older than seventeen or eighteen. She had Charge's gray eyes. Something in the chin looked familiar, too.

She flipped the photo over.

In the same handwriting as the letter, the words "Ed's first victim" were written.

"No." It couldn't be. The blood in her veins chilled. The photo slipped from her hand and fell to the hardwood floor.

Emily covered her mouth. She'd known that Ed had a girlfriend before her. She'd found a photo up in the attic, buried under some old clothes, right after she'd married him on a whim because she'd been too desperate for attention from any living soul to see him for who he was.

For a few short months, he was her prince charming, making her feel important and loved. He took her dancing, he brought her flowers, he looked at her with what she'd thought was love. She told herself that her unlucky streak was over and to trust her heart. She'd finally found a home. But soon after, she started to see another side of him, and the day she'd found that photo was the first time he hit her. Not the last.

"Nosy bitches, the both of you," he'd said, referring to herself and the woman in the photo.

She's Ed's ex…

Emily picked up the photo again and stared at those sweet, kind eyes looking back. She didn't know who this woman was to Charge—his sister? A friend's daughter? It didn't matter, really. What did was that this girl had been Ed's first victim. What mattered was that the girl meant something to Charge—enough that he had a photo.

How in the world did I end up in El Paso, working with Charge? What were the odds that she'd land on *his* doorstep? That he'd be a hit man who knew who she was? That they *would* have a vendetta against the same person?

Emily set the photo on the bed and scrubbed her face with her palms. *This is crazy.* He'd known all along about their connection but decided not to tell her. There had to be a reason.

She stared into the dark, empty fireplace. *He didn't need me to kill Ed. He never did. He had the men, the guns, and the ability all along. So why wait until now to take Ed out?*

The only reasonable explanation had to do with "the rules." Charge believed in them, one being to never use the team for personal vendettas or greed.

"Charge…" He should have said something. Of course, what was there to say? That fate or luck had intervened and brought them together? She didn't believe in that crap, but it made her think of something her dad used to say: *"Baby, sometimes life hands you lemons. Sometimes, it hands you sweet juicy apples, but when you see fingers, don't ask why."*

She never understood what he meant until now. The fingers were attached to a hand, and when life offered one, it was best to be thankful. Bottom line, this detour to El Paso, to suite forty-five, had turned out to be more than just a pit stop on a very difficult journey. For the very first time since her aunt Mary had died, Emily felt like someone was looking out for her, telling her not to lose faith in this world.

Yeah. Well, we'll see if I'm right. If she was, Charge would come through that door and tell her she was safe. Forever.

God, please let him come back. Please...

CHAPTER SIXTEEN

Ten days. Ten days of hell. Ten days of hand-washing her horrible pink outfit. Ten days of pacing the two-bedroom cabin. Ten days of resisting her phone to search the news. Ten days of playing with Charge's stupid AM/FM radio, hoping to hear anything going on in the outside world. Ten days of canned vegetables and frozen pizzas left in Charge's freezer.

Today was the deadline. Charge said if he didn't come back, she was supposed to take the gun, the money, and the contents of the envelope, which she'd refused to open. She refused to accept defeat.

But now it was time. He hadn't come. He hadn't called. *Something went wrong. I can feel it.*

"Screw it!" She went to the drawer and pulled out the gun and money, setting them both on the butcherblock counter. She took the envelope and opened it. Inside was a bus ticket north and a ferry ticket to a place in Alaska. There was also a set of keys with a paper tag and an address attached.

The note inside simply said, *Good luck.*

Oh my God. Her heart felt like it'd hit the floor. This was it? This was how it all ended?

No. Fuck this. She got out her phone and started scanning the online news in Jersey, careful not to search anything in particular.

Nothing. Not a word about shoot-outs or prostitution busts. Nothing about a missing FBI agent or a manhunt.

Sour notes strummed inside her stomach. The lack of news could mean Charge and the team had been killed. It could also mean they did the job, and Ed and his team had been wiped off the face of the earth but no one noticed them missing yet. What worried her most, however, was the fact that Charge hadn't returned.

She hung her head. There was no way to know for sure, but she knew she couldn't wait here to find out the truth. Charge could have been captured and tortured for information. Ed would want to know who'd sent him.

She put the items Charge had left into her purse, except for the photo. That went into the pocket of her pink hoodie. She felt obligated to keep it safe for him. Whoever Ed's ex was, she held a place in Charge's heart.

Emily opened the front door and froze, staring down the pine-tree-lined dirt road. Walking away felt like giving up. It felt like accepting defeat and saying that those women's lives didn't matter. Justice didn't matter. Helping Charge didn't matter.

She didn't know how long she stood there debating over going back to El Paso to find out what had happened—to the place where she might track down the team. All she knew was everything inside her fought. To leave like this simply felt like running towards a coward's life.

Emily slipped the photo of Ed's ex-girlfriend from her pocket. Charge had known how hard it would be for her to walk away, but he'd also wanted her to know that if he died, it was for the girl in this photo. Emily was obliged to make some sort of meaning from it all.

She sighed and stepped outside, closing the door behind her.

Emily sat at the small bus terminal next to the laundromat and gas station, where weekend campers and logging trucks pulled off for fuel, snacks, or ice. And to wash clothes, apparently.

She checked the bus route number shown on her ticket. It would take her north to Albuquerque, then on to Denver, where she would have to change buses to get to Seattle. The trip would take four days total, excluding the one-day ferry ride to Alaska—to some small fishing town north of Ketchikan, called Wrangell, which was inaccessible by car.

Honestly, none of this felt real. Her mind was still back in that cabin, waiting for things to finally be set right. That was the path she was supposed to be on. That was the life she could see so clearly in her head. *Not this.*

She cracked open a Diet Pepsi and sat back against the plexiglass of the bus stop. It was starting to sprinkle right in the middle of June.

She pulled the pink hoodie from the plastic grocery bag she'd used to carry her few belongings. Funny how she looked like a penniless drifter, even though she had ten thousand dollars cash on her person—thanks to Charge's generosity, which she'd never understand, since the first twenty K was still back in her studio, waiting for the landlord to discover.

Suddenly, a dark blue pickup truck with tinted windows pulled in front of the bus stop. Maybe someone being dropped off?

But no one got out.

Shit. She slid her hand into her shopping bag just as the window on the passenger side lowered.

Two cool gray eyes looked back at her.

"Oh my God!" She jumped up and grabbed her stuff. "What the hell happened to you?"

"Get in. We need to talk." Charge's dark brows were furrowed with intense emotion, and his lips, framed by a thick black wash of stubble, were set in a firm line. He had dark circles under his eyelids, like he hadn't slept in days, and the whites of his eyes were red. If she didn't know any better, she'd say he'd been... *No. Impossible. Guys like him don't cry.*

Whatever the case, something was wrong.

She hopped inside, resisting the urge to make assumptions. Or throw her arms around him. "I thought I'd never see you again."

He grunted something and pulled around to the back of the building, out of sight from the main road.

She was on pins and needles. "Charge? Are you okay?"

He left the engine running and stared out the windshield at nothing. "Ed killed himself," he said quietly.

"What?"

"The moment we stormed your house, he locked himself in the bathroom. He must've heard us coming."

What a coward. Couldn't even face his death like a man. "So he took himself out. I bet you found him cowering in the bathtub."

"Something like that."

"And the rest of his men?" she asked.

"Done. Dealt with it."

"So…it's over." She let out a slow breath. She could hardly believe it.

"Yes. And as far as anyone's concerned, he and his men fell off the face of the earth. Job was done clean and completely successful."

"And the women?" She stared at the side of his face, eagerly searching for any sign of good news.

"There were only eighteen, but we took them to a friend of mine. He has ties in the State Department and will ensure they get assistance and see their families again."

Two women had died since she'd left. Her heart went out to them, but that was not on her. Ed and his crew did that.

Emily let out a sigh of relief. Was it really over? *It is. I'm free. I'm fucking free!* "Did anyone get hurt?" She referred to his team.

Charge blinked and finally turned his cold gaze on her. "Not yet."

She jerked her head back. She wasn't following.

"The money, Emily. The money," he said.

"Oh no…" She tilted her head and stared at the ceiling of the truck. *Selfish fucking coward.* Ed died before anyone could talk to him. "The team didn't get paid."

Charge was silent, but she felt an ominous shift inside the pickup. The hairs on the back of her neck rose. From the periphery of her vision, she could see Charge's left hand shoved down near the edge of his left thigh, next to the driver's side door.

"You're going to shoot me, aren't you?" she asked, not bothering to look at him. In her heart, she knew that was what he had to do, and it wasn't negotiable. A deal was a deal. There were rules. "Couldn't they have at least sent someone else and just done it without me knowing it was coming?"

"I wanted it to be me—someone who knows you."

"Oh," she muttered quietly, the shock of the moment feeling completely surreal. He didn't want her to die alone. "I'd run, but I'm pretty sure you'd put two bullets in my head before I opened the door. Plus, it's very thoughtful of you to make sure I knew what happened with the job. Thank you. I can die in peace, and that means a lot." She finally turned her head and looked him in the eyes.

The cold grays weren't so cold anymore. There was a sadness in them.

"You remind me of her," he said softly.

"Of who?"

"My sister—the one Ed killed," he replied solemnly.

Ah. So that's who she was. "Now that Ed is gone, I hope it brings you peace." She sighed. "If it's any consolation, he was a very good con man.

I'm sure she was smart—smarter than me, anyway. She didn't marry him."

His dark brows furrowed. "But *she* never had the common sense to run from him. You did."

Charged stared at her, the two of them locking eyes.

Emily understood she would never really know Charge or what thoughts brewed in the dark corners of his mind, but she was grateful it would be his face she'd be seeing last, and not Ed's. Charge had seen something in her that had made her stop feeling like a victim. He'd pushed her and made her feel strong. For a few short moments, she got to know what it was like to be the hero. Yes, the situations had been fake— Charge needing help, freeing that hostage—but her responses weren't. When push came to shove, she stepped up, and now she knew what she was made of. *I am not weak. I am not nothing. Ed was wrong.* And now she could die being completely free of him.

Emily leaned forward and pressed her mouth to Charge's soft, full lips. He didn't flinch or push her away, but he didn't kiss her back either. No matter. The kiss wasn't about that. She simply wanted him to know she forgave him and understood. Killing took something from a person. She got that now. She simply didn't want to put another dent in his soul.

She pulled away, faced forward, and closed

her eyes. "I'm ready."

She waited and heard a click. She made fists with her hands, bracing for the pain. Her heartbeat was so loud she swore the truck's windows were vibrating.

But then…nothing.

She opened her eyes to find Charge with the gun in his lap, but he wasn't looking at her. The photo of his sister was in his hand. It must've dropped from her hoodie when she'd slid inside the pickup.

He stared at the thing for several long moments. Not a word. And somehow she knew he'd changed his mind. Maybe his loyalty to the team and his rules were outweighed by other things.

Finally, he spoke. "Take the ticket and get on the bus. You'll be safe in Wrangell. For a while, at least. Then I'd consider getting lost in Canada. Maybe head to Europe after a few years."

"What if the team finds out you let me leave?"

"They won't. I'll tell them you'd already taken off. I never saw you."

She frowned. She didn't want to die, but she didn't want to live on the run the rest of her life, either. "Isn't there another way? I didn't deceive anyone. Ed died before you could get the location of the money."

"Your end of the deal wasn't held up. They don't care why—they're hired guns, not a charity."

"Okay. What if I go back and try to work it out? What if I offer to repay them?"

"With what? You have no job. And you have no hope of ever making that kind of money. Ed might be dead, but sooner or later, people will start asking questions about his disappearance, and yours. They'll be waiting for either of you to resurface."

Meaning she might be free of her husband, but she would always have to look over her shoulder and lie low. That meant taking low-paying jobs where people didn't ask too many questions.

"The only two options," he added, "are for you to get on that bus or take the job."

"Take the job? You mean *your* job."

"Yes. You're off-limits if you're part of the team. Also, they might be willing to forgive you if you work hard and give them your share of the fees for a year or two—until the million is paid back with interest."

Her jaw dropped. "This was your plan all along, wasn't it? You wanted to back me into a corner."

"No, Emily!" he let loose. "My plan was to offer you my role once you passed the tests. Then I'd train you and leave. And if you recall, *you* were the one who begged for a chance to convince the team to do that job. It wasn't my *fucking* idea, and neither were the terms of the *fucking* arrangement!" He balled his hands into frustrated fists. "I'm just—I'm *trying* to give you an out!" He slammed his fists on the steering wheel.

She whooshed out a breath, taking an emotional step back. Seeing him like this shook her foundation. Did he really care about her life so much?

The answer made her more determined than ever to run. She didn't want to repeat history. Ed had been able to lure her into his dark, violent life because she'd trusted him. She'd believed he cared about her. *Never again.*

"I can't take the job," she said. "I don't want to live in that world and ki-kill people for a living, no matter how bad they are."

He shook his head with disapproval. "I never took you for a coward."

"I'm not a coward just because I don't want to be a lion. I don't have it in me. You were wrong."

"Well then, that leaves you one option," he said curtly.

"I'm sorry, Charge. And I'm really grateful for everything."

Without looking at her, he nodded, jaw pulsing. "Better hurry, then. You'll miss your bus."

"Goodbye." She popped the door handle.

He reached in his pocket and produced a piece of paper with a number. "Call me if you change your mind. Good luck."

CHAPTER SEVENTEEN

Around two in the morning, the bus arrived in Denver. The passengers unloaded, most heading inside the small terminal to buy food or use the bathrooms. Her connecting bus wouldn't be departing until five a.m.

She stood outside for a few moments, inhaling the cool Colorado night air, twisting her back and trying to coax the blood back into her legs.

She'd hoped to have some sort of epiphany during the seven-hour drive, but mostly she'd slept and tried not to think about how things ended: badly. She'd be on the run for the rest of her life.

Still, one thing had come out of all this: She'd learned that in even the darkest of places, a person could still find goodness. Charge taught her that. His soul was scarred and barren, yet even his frosty heart still managed to beat. If there was hope for him, there was hope for her to find her way back and trust people again.

Emily's stomach grumbled with *the hope* of sustenance, so she went inside the nearly empty terminal. It had high ceilings, and several rows of green plastic chairs all pointed toward a TV set to the news. The convenience store in the corner was brightly lit, and a security guard stood chatting with a female clerk behind the register. Emily went inside, grabbing a bag of chips, a water, and a small sandwich. Engrossed in their flirty conversation, the two didn't even bother looking at her when she paid.

Looks like security is busy securing himself a booty call for later.

She hit the bathroom, hanging her stuff on the back of the second stall door. Once done, she reached for her pink hoodie, but it slipped and fell onto the dirty bathroom floor.

Gross. And there was nowhere to wash it.

She bent down to pick it up, but when she reached, she noticed a pair of big black boots in the stall next to her. Right in front of those was a pair of women's white sneakers. Both pairs of shoes were facing the same way.

Yuck. They're having sex in this nasty place. God only knew what a person could catch here. But then why weren't they moving? Why weren't they making fucking noises?

That's weird.

She grabbed her stuff and heard a muted whimper.

Emily froze again. *That did not sound like a happy whimper.*

She slid her gun from her shopping bag and opened the door, going to the sink to run the water. She hit the air dryer and tiptoed over to the stall again, standing up on the toilet. She peeked over the divider. A man with blond hair and tattoos on his arms held a knife to a woman's throat from behind. He was fumbling with the back of her pants.

Jesus.

Emily carefully stepped down from the toilet. She wanted to tell him to drop the knife, but what if he slit the woman's throat? What if he turned it around and said, "No. You drop the gun, or I'll kill her"?

Emily glanced up at the ceiling. *This fucker, this disgusting animal...* He probably deserved to die—at least more than that woman—so why the hesitation?

Her mind flashed to Marco and the test. The feeling she'd experienced after pulling the trigger hadn't been guilt. She'd only been worried about the woman. That, and Emily felt pissed off about having to kill Marco at all. Doing it meant giving up a piece of herself, of her innocence, and frankly it just felt wrong; a worthless animal shouldn't be allowed to take away something so precious. Or a life. All in all, however, none of those emotions had superseded the good of knowing she'd helped someone. Yes, it all turned out to be fake, but maybe Charge had given her that test for a reason. It was the gift of knowing what she was made of.

And whether I'm a lion or a gazelle.

It took Emily a second to decide. She stepped back up on the toilet, looked down at the man, and pressed the gun to the back of his head. "Hey. Asshole."

A day later, Emily stepped out of the semi, thanking the truck driver for the ride. It was funny, but she'd never hitchhiked before—lots of psychos and killers out there. But now it was her they should be afraid of. Lions were dangerous.

She shut the truck's door, feeling the hot, moist El Paso air stuffing her lungs. "God, I hate the humidity."

She walked over to the bus stop, sat down on the bench, and popped a piece of mint gum into her mouth. *I hope for once I'm doing the right thing.* Only time would tell.

She got out her cell, hit SEND, and waited for that deep, unfeeling voice to answer. "Hey. It's Emily. I'm in."

THE PAUSE

Want an Alert for Book #2?

OPTION #1: Hope that M.O.'s enemies are tracking your reading habits and disclose this information to you in a timely fashion.
Success Rate: 0%

OPTION #2: Stalk M.O. on Facebook and hope the FB spy-bots bless you with an announcement.
Success Rate: 10%

OPTION #3: Stalk M.O. on Instagram and hope M.O. floats to the top of your feed.
Success Rate: 20%

OPTION #4: Sign up for M.O.'s release alerts and perhaps learn the author's true identity. (Ha! Never!) But most definitely, you will hear about book 2 before everyone else.
Success Rate: 100% (Okay. It's really like 99% but whatever. It's the best chance you've got! And M.O. is way too busy writing to spam you, so there's that.)

SIGN UP HERE

M.O.

MACK

Find out about upcoming M.O. Mack releases, regardless of probability, by following or signing up here.

FACEBOOK

www.facebook.com/Author-MO-Mack-111698477219966

INSTAGRAM

www.instagram.com/author_mo_mack

NEWSLETTER

mailchi.mp/c9a3e31062ee/author-mo-mack-news

PINTEREST

www.pinterest.com/Author_MO_Mack

www.authormomack.com

www.ingramcontent.com/pod-product-compliance
Lightning Source LLC
Chambersburg PA
CBHW071936150726
47999CB00001B/223